A HISTORY OF THE MIDDLE EASTside

*

Jonathon Narvey

WRITEIMAGE

Creative Commons Cover illustration by Jillian Anne Lopez-
Stemwede, Artists4Israel

For information or purchase address:
WRITEIMAGE, #202 – 111 West 10th Avenue, Vancouver,
British Columbia, Canada V5Y 1R7
www.writeimage.ca

First edition

Canadian Cataloguing in Publication Data
Narvey, Jonathon
A History Of The Middle Eastside
ISBN 978-0-9737333-1-0

PROLOGUE
1894

THE YID

It was a long way down from the roof to the street. Felix' crew had Alfred cornered up there. It wasn't looking good for the Yid.

"I didn't do it," Alfred protested. "You got it all wrong." He was backed up against the ledge. Five of them had him surrounded.

Six storeys down. That height wouldn't just break bones. They'd be scraping him off the sidewalk.

"If you didn't do it, why'd you run, Yid?" Felix demanded. "We know you sold out to the other gang. We got the proof."

Alfred didn't see the point in trying to reason with this lot.

He'd run out because he'd seen Felix heading his way with his trusty steel bat in his hand. Plus, Felix had threatened to kill him a few minutes before that. Alfred didn't have a gun, or enough bullets to deal with all of Felix' minions even if he was packing. So the running was actually the easiest part to understand.

Perhaps a more aggressive approach would yield results. "Proof? You got jack-shit," Alfred yelled at them at the top of his lungs. "Henry's got it in for me. He's telling lies. And you're a fool to believe him."

In fact, Henry was the thug who had actually sold out to the other gang. This unknown fact would not help Alfred on the roof, though.

Felix shook his head. "Henry's my best thug. You never should have come to this part of Central Station, Alfred. You Yids can't be trusted. You're all liars and snakes. And your crew should never should have left the Middle Eastside for this neighborhood."

2

The others had murder in their eyes. They started closing in on Alfred.

Alfred switched to pleading for his life. He reminded them of how he'd fought alongside them in countless dust-ups with the other gangs of the borough. They'd shared fights and drinks and awful jokes around a card table. But none of that mattered now.

The gangsters grabbed him. He struggled. He stopped trying to bargain with them and just begged for his life.

He could have saved his breath.

"Wait!" Theo shouted at the men on the roof. He'd just run up the stairs and burst out of the pillbox-type entrance. He'd heard Alfred's shouts from the street. "Stop what you're doing!"

"Damn it," Felix cursed. "Theo, this is settled. You got no reason to be here. We're going to finish this."

Theo was doubled over and puffing loudly. He'd bounded up the stairs and his lungs were practically bursting. "You got no cause for this Felix. You don't know Alfred was the one."

"Now you're taking his side?" Felix asked. "What, were you two in on it together?"

"Go fuck yourself, Felix," Theo shouted. "There's no conspiracy here. You just want to kill someone."

Felix wasn't letting up. "He's a Yid. We can't trust him. He must have done it. And if you try to stop me, I'm going to throw your ass off this roof, too, Theo."

Theo backed off. He'd tried. But he couldn't stop this from happening.

"Throw him down, boys!" Felix ordered.

Alfred stopped trying to fight back at the end. Theo thought that was the worst part. When the men pushed Alfred off the ledge, he didn't try to push back. He didn't shout any more. He just went.

When Alfred's head hit the pavement, his skull caved in. He died instantly. The gutter was a total mess.

"Clean that shit up," Felix ordered his crew. "Theo, you go with them. Get that dead Yid off our street. It's a disgrace."

3

Theo went with them. He helped cart the body off on a stretcher for the layabout blue-collar fish to take care of it. He even helped hose down the pavement until all the blood had run down into the sewer where no one could ever see it.

The next day, Theo took his girlfriend down to the train station and the two unobtrusive Yids made their way to the Middle Eastside.

He would never come back to Central Station for as long as he lived.

PART 1
1948

1

NIGHT OF THE LIVING DEAD

It was still pitch-dark outside when the gangster known throughout the Middle Eastside as Uncle Herzl was woken up by a knock on the front door of the Citadel Hotel.

At first, he tried to ignore it. He looked to his bedside table. The clock showed five thirty-two in the morning.

None of his people would knock at such an hour. Big Ben's flunkies weren't coming by for their money this week.

And Fariq's crew wouldn't bother to knock.

Herzl turned over and closed his eyes. He began dreaming pleasantly once more of the time he'd boned his chubby piano teacher back in the long-lost years of his youth.

Knock, knock.

Again, with the knocking.

The stranger at the door surely understood all too well the boastful foolishness of announcing one's presence at a time when the world was supposed to be unconscious.

Herzl descended the stairs in a robe and slippers, stroking his heavy beard. He gripped a loaded Smith and Wesson revolver in his big pocket.

Where the hell was that lumpy waste of space, Boaz? Dreaming of cheese blintzes and greasy chicken legs, no doubt. Absolutely no use as a night watchman. Barely serviceable as a shlammer. Chernik was likewise out of it, probably sleeping off a couple fingers of cheap scotch.

No, there would be no cavalry coming.

It was impossible to get good help in this neighborhood. Herzl would handle this business on his own.

He stood behind the wall to the side of the door just in case it was one of Fariq's shtarkes. The bastards could be just waiting to open up from behind the door with a shotgun or grenades capable of breaching the reinforced entrance.

"Who's out there?" Herzl asked in a grumpy snarl. "Be warned, I'm heavily armed and you just woke me from a filthy dream. I'm in no mood."

"Uncle Herzl," a hollow, ghostly rasp answered. "It's Zev Polanski, from Central Station. Open the door."

"That's impossible," Herzl fired back. "The Polanski's are all dead."

"Not yet," the hollow voice answered. "But if you don't open this door, the last of them will freeze to death on your doorstep. Now open up, you old shammes."

Herzl hesitated. It could be a trick.

But then again, Fariq's men would have probably just tried to shoot him through the front door by now.

Herzl flicked on the light and looked through the little latch, his hidden weapon pointing into the darkness. His knees buckled at the sight of the wretched corpse that stood in the doorway, staring at him with all the humanity of rotten death.

He opened the door to get a look at this thing that went by the name Polanski.

The thing stood like a man. It was dressed like a man, though his black suit was rumpled and greasy like he'd just crawled out of a sewer.

A streak of dried blood ran from the forehead of his close-cropped cranium down to his filthy shirt collar. In his right hand, this wraith held an ancient Colt revolver. For now, it was pointed at the ground.

"Uncle Herzl," the corpse pleaded, shivering from the cold so violently that it's skeletal frame threatened to collapse in on itself then and there. "Let me in. You got no idea what it took for me to get here. No fucking idea."

Herzl kept his finger on the trigger. The full horror of what he was seeing was only beginning to drip it's way into his brain.

"Zev Polanski?" he croaked. "Kid, is it really you? Get the hell in here, you little son of a bitch."

The impossibly thin shadow of a man wavered unsteadily. Somehow it managed to remain upright, putting one foot in front of the other to gain entrance to Herzl's living room.

"What's going on? Who's there?"

It was Boaz, standing in the hall with his shotgun leveled at the upright dead man who called himself Zev Polanski. His eyes were wide with unease. "Who the hell is this?" Boaz muttered.

"Put your weapon down, you useless excuse for a shlammer," Herzl commanded. Now he noticed Boaz's wife Zedorah in the hallway.

"It's Herschel Polanski's kid. Go make yourself useful and heat up some soup for our guest. And put some coffee on. It's going to be a long night."

The visitor was brought into the kitchen. The black coffee steamed just as the first red aura of sunset filtered through the barred window.

Now Boaz and Zedorah's daughter Rivkah had joined them, along with her new husband, Chernik the trigger-man. The young lady with the red hair observed in silence, understanding only that some kind of ghost had settled in their home and was helping himself to a bowl of greasy chicken broth.

A little flicker of light seemed to have ignited within the visitor's dead eyes.

"Good soup," Zev grunted. "I haven't eaten in days."

"So you got out of Central Station," Herzl continued. "Are there more, kid?"

Zev shrugged. "Some, and they're on the way. Not many. The ones that made it, they're mostly coming here. Washington's taking in some. Not too many. It was easier to get into the Middle Eastside. But only just."

"What's Big Ben doing?" Herzl asked.

"Scumbag sure didn't make it easy," Zev answered. "Any of the crew he catches, he turns 'em right back to the old hood for Ivan to deal with. Who knows what that old bastard's doing with 'em."

Herzl turned to Boaz and Chernik. "Get your crew together. Take the route to Central Station. You need to get

8

there before Fariq's men see what's what. They'll hang these Yids from the lamp-posts if they see 'em."

Boaz hesitated, eyeing their new acquaintance. Herzl poked the big shtarke in the neck. That got him going. The black-suited bulk instantly vanished from the room.

Herzl turned to continue with his visitor, but Zev had gone silent. He stared blankly at the wall.

The kid could have been dead, except for the barest movement of his chest that showed he was still breathing.

"Is he going to make it?" Rivkah asked Uncle Herzl. The big man had forgotten Boaz and Zedorah's daughter was still in the room.

"We'll see, young lady," Herzl answered. "You scared?"

"A little," she admitted.

"Well, maybe we should be. We'll see soon enough."

He was right.

Herzl watched as Boaz and his crew returned to the Citadel Hotel with more of the walking wounded from Central Station. "They don't even know they're coming the frying pan to the fire. Someone has to tell them. These poor schnooks."

The crew scoured the routes from Central Station and managed to pick up a dozen of these cruel specimens. One of the men Boaz rescued from the improvised bed of a slimy gutter expired in the car. They dumped the body on the side of the road just two hundred yards before getting past one of Big Ben's checkpoints.

Lazy shmucks just waved them on.

A few more of the shell-shocked Polanski crew shlammers managed to get to the Citadel Hotel under their own power. Half of them would not last out the week. They were already too far gone.

Poor schnooks.

Maybe they were all ferkakdeh.

2

WALKING WOUNDED

The beaten-down survivors had been through hell. The more that came out, the more unreal it seemed that these pitiful specimens had emerged from Central Station.

The last couple of months had seen a confusing and complicated series of provocations and double crosses turn into the most destructive gang war ever in Central Station.

How had it all started? As usual, it was the small differences and greedy zero-sum ambitions between the gangs that caused the most trouble.

There'd been a long blood feud between Gruber's brownshirts and the Polanski crew. It ebbed and flowed over generations. Fact was that Herschel Polanski's gang had always held a precarious position in Central Station even at the best of times.

They'd never really had the numbers to match Gruber's operation, or the turf that Ivan's gang had amassed on the Upper Eastside. To leverage his meager assets, Polanski had managed to build up connections among some of the key lieutenants in the various territories; some say he even had some pull with Washington in the Upper Westside.

These connections never really amounted to much, though. All they did was infuriate Gruber to no end.

And the rest of Central Station wasn't much more hospitable for Herschel Polanski's business. All the other bosses resented Polanski's mucking about in their operations. Pretty much any profits Herschel made went straight into protection money to all concerned parties. Even with the bribes, Polanski's people ended up with busted faces and broken legs at a higher per capita rate than was customary for the City's gangsters.

The breaking point came.

And when it did, it was brutal.

Gruber saw a chance to move against Big Ben and Francois, and most of all, his arch-rival Ivan. He'd been running a weapons-smuggling operation. None of the other bosses even had a clue how big it was.

Gruber was always one for swagger and boasting. This maybe made it easier for him to hide the extent of his build-up right in plain sight.

The balance of power had changed, not just in Central Station. For the whole City.

First, though, he'd have to knock off Polanski's crew for good. Rumor had it that Gruber set up one of his own shtarkes for a false-flag hit blamed on Polanski.

Gruber's gang, really more of an army at this point, stormed Polanski's hideout.

Overnight, Polanski's gang practically got wiped out. Depending on who you talked to, Polanski himself might have died in a running battle with Gruber's top guns. Another rumor was that he was kept in a cage and tortured for weeks before he finally bled to death.

The rest of Polanski's crew didn't fare much better.

Those that got out of Central Station before Gruber's power play were just putting off the inevitable.

Gruber had made a deal with Ivan before the crackdown on Polanski's crew. He knew the Upper Eastside's boss was too chicken to refuse.

So Ivan just watched as Gruber swallowed up most of Polanski's turf. Then he moved in and grabbed the rest for himself. The deal was done.

Soon as Gruber had his ducks lined up, Francois and Big Ben were next.

Gruber's armored cars and disciplined jackboots swarmed into Francois' turf. It didn't take long. He gave the remainder of Francois' gang the choice of joining forces. Any of Polanski's people that had escaped into Francois' turf did not last long after that.

Big Ben's shlammers still held out in their little corner of Central Station. But the main turf war in that part of the City was pretty much done.

Francois had rolled over faster than anyone had ever expected. Some say this emboldened Gruber. But his next move was probably inevitable.

Ivan was always Gruber's main target, even before he took out Polanski.

Ivan was the big boss of the Upper Eastside and he had his fingers in everything: smack, guns, prostitution, all kinds of smuggling in every corner of the City. He had a reputation as the kind of boss that would erase his best enforcers on just a hint of a suspicion of disloyalty. But even that sort of ruthlessness wasn't enough to keep Gruber at bay. It may even have provoked him.

When Gruber made his move into the Upper Westside, Ivan's key lieutenants were all six feet under. Ivan's operations were all a shambles from mismanagement.

Gruber threw everything he had at Ivan. Guns. Bombs. Armored cars. And the best trigger-men money could buy.

His sheer bloody-mindedness paid dividends at first. Ivan's people pulled back on all fronts. They abandoned the power company and the east warehouse district almost without a fight.

And as usual, wherever Gruber found Polanski's dead-enders that had managed to squeeze out a shadow of an existence on Ivan's turf, they ended up dead, too.

The invaders didn't treat the rest of Ivan's people much better. Even under the paranoid boss's iron grip, the Upper Eastside had never seen so much blood.

Ivan was on his last legs. Some said even his inner circle was looking at doing him themselves. They were hoping to at least get a deal with Gruber like Francois had got, to save their own necks.

Ivan's solution for their backsliding was to send them off to the meat-packing district to go toe-to-toe with Gruber's butchers.

The City was burning everywhere. The streets of the Upper Eastside were running three inches thick with blood and guts.

But now the war that Gruber had started began to turn against him.

Ivan's forces were fighting with their backs to the wall. But they were still fighting. Big Ben was still in the game as well, just barely. His sharpshooters managed to keep enough of Gruber's shtarkes pinned down in Francois' turf. It prevented an all-out assault on the Royal Westminster Club.

Gruber's forces were too spread out on both fronts to finish off either of his main enemies.

No one knows what made Gruber pull the switch that ensured his doom. He knew that Washington was supplying Big Ben with the ammunition that was keeping his jackboots on their heels. He also had to know that taking on the boss of the Upper Westside would be suicide.

Maybe his confidence had been bolstered when some of his squads managed to take out a few of Washington's ammo convoys without triggering a response. Maybe he figured Washington just didn't have the stomach for it.

But When Gruber declared war on Washington, it was game over.

With his gleaming white teeth and immaculate movie-star hair, you might take Washington for a bit of a fancy boy.

Sure, he's vain. But he will stick his fist down your throat, tear out your liver and show it to you. And then he'll really start hurting you.

Washington came in from his side with ten thousand guns blazing. He let Big Ben tag along just enough so his feelings didn't get hurt. Meanwhile, Ivan rolled up all of the turf that Gruber had taken from him. The enforcers from the Upper Westside burned and blasted every one of Gruber's henchmen they could find.

Soon enough, the allied gangs were pounding away at Gruber on his home turf. Even Francois and his treacherous thugs got back into it as Gruber's jackboots fled for the Bunker.

Gruber took his own life just as the other gangs shot their way into the Bunker. And that was it.

His gang was finished. The conquerors divided up Central Station among themselves.

Now they just had to clean up the stinking smoky ruins at the center of the City.

Then something happened that caught the survivors by surprise. Out of the smoking ruins of Gruber's broken territory, remnants of Polanski's gang miraculously emerged.

They didn't look much like gangsters. Not even fish, really. They were starving. Dead on their feet. Most of them, you had to really look at for a while before you figured out they were actually living, breathing human beings.

Some would make their way to Washington's turf. He grudgingly allowed them in. He figured if they'd survived this long, they might be inventive enough to deliver some kind of percentage eventually.

Meanwhile, another contingent of the survivors were conscripted into Ivan's gang.

For the rest of Polanski's diminished crew of hard-done-by Yids, there was only one place left to go from Central Station. The Middle Eastside.

The Yids had longstanding blood ties to the Middle Eastside. Today, that was where Big Ben ran some of his side rackets. But a long while back, most of these toughs had got kicked out. That was what came out of a neighborhood turf war just as cataclysmic as the more recent bloodbath in Central Station.

A few Yids remained. Mostly, they were now holed up at the Citadel Hotel with Herzl.

Living with this forgotten remnant of invisible losers was far preferable to dying in the hopeless violence in Central Station he'd long predicted.

Death isn't a stranger to gangsters. But those who rise to the position of boss know that there's little profit in it.

Now, as he watched the walking wounded descend upon this final refuge, he knew that it wouldn't be long before the other gangs in the Middle Eastside would do something about it. This single-file train of skinny little bastards with the bad teeth and hollow eyes were going to change things in the Middle Eastside. And the others weren't going to like it.

War was coming.

14

3
NO MORE PROTECTION

Zev looked around Herzl's office. It was dusty with filing cabinets and piles of clutter that might have been there for years. Possibly the world's very first couch took up the back corner, stained by coffee, cigar ashes and sundry sources of human sweat.

Like the rest of the Citadel Hotel, it overflowed with the ancient cracked furnishings and fixtures of generations past. An ornate eight-armed candelabra that couldn't possibly be made of real gold took up most of the real estate on the mantle over the fireplace. Moldy books and yellowed papers cluttered Herzl's desk.

The place reeked of broken ambitions and failed dreams.

"I knew your father, Zev," Uncle Herzl began. "Good man. It's a shame what happened to him.

"You're tough like him, you know. So few made it out of Central Station. To get to my door on your own two feet... well, you've got brass balls, kid. But I guess you're feeling now like you've gone from the frying pan into the fire."

Zev looked out the window at the broad building to the south of the Citadel Hotel. The squat fortress-like building was a ruin. It was topped by the Asqua Club, a favored stronghold for Fariq's goons. No Yid could get close to the place.

Uncle Herzl did not get up from the desk in his office. "You know what's behind the Wall."

Zev shrugged. "That's David the Butcher's old digs. Before the Muj boarded it up."

"That meshugener ruled here once," Herzl added. "Toughest gangster in the five boroughs.

"The Muj say he ground up his enemies into sausage. Feh. That's a vile slur. He was a real boss. Best of 'em. He set down the first laws of the streets and you better believe no one

15

piddled around on his watch. Gangster and fish. They'd come from all around to pay their respect to him."

"Time's have changed," Zev noted.

"The perks aren't quite the same as when the old man was in charge," Herzl replied, a little wistfully.

"You think there's anything left in there?" Polanski asked.

Herzl shook his head. "Look at how the Muj have let the place rot. You can see from here. Of course, no one really knows what's in those ruins except the Muj, since they covered it up with the Asqua Club. Probably, they're using it as a toilet."

"Fucking shmendriks," Zev replied. "What a neighborhood."

Herzl frowned. "Not much alternative. You know why I came down here from Central Station in the first place, kid? Anyone told you?"

Polanski shrugged.

"Much of my youth was misspent schmoozing around Central Station. I spent a little time with Francois' crew back when he was just coming up. Long before Gruber ever came on to the scene.

"There was this other Yid gangster who liked to schmooze there, too. I didn't know him. Not well. But this Yid, he got accused of working against Francois' interests.

"There was no proof. There hardly ever is in these cases. But this time it was really fluff. A lot of Francois' shlammers even figured they knew the real guy who did the deed... something about cutting in one of the other gangs on some racket or another. I don't even remember the details."

"So what happened to the Yid?" Polanski asked.

"What do you think?" Herzl asked. "He gut hung out to dry. Literally. Off the ledge of a tall building. I saw it happen with my own two eyes. The Yid hit the pavement head-first and collapsed into himself like an accordion. What a mess.

"My buddies in Francois' crew, they didn't even know I was a Yid. But I realized then that Central Station was no place for us. It was a beautiful part of the City. You remember from when you were younger, kid. But we couldn't stay for the

16

scenery. Gruber might not have been around yet, but I knew it would be only a matter of time before him or someone like him came around."

Polanski nodded. "My father stuck it out. Looks like you were right in the end, Herzl."

Herzl changed the subject. "So the Yids from Central Station still know the old stories."

"Sure," Zev replied, staring at his shoes. "And I catch some of the old-timers from your outfit looking at the Butcher Shop sometimes. They get this odd look. Like they're remembering something. Though none of your boys have ever been there, I take it."

Herzl lit his pipe, breathing in the acrid tobacco with grim satisfaction. "I've been here long enough. I get that look, too. Stay here long enough, we all do it."

"Big Ben could have turned that place over to your crew ages ago. He's taken enough of your protection money."

"Nasser's bitch babysits it for him," Herzl exhaled, breathing blue smoke across the room. "No way he was ever going to just give it away. And we can't even get close to it. Not while we've got five rusty gats for this whole operation. This gang has got problems, I tell you."

He took a long puff of his pipe. "Now, your old digs are just a turf war waiting to happen. Washington and Ivan are bound to go toe-to-toe one of these days. They'll level everything that's not already dust. Nothing there for Yids anymore. Maybe nothing for us here, either."

"As bad as all that, eh, Herzl?"

"Worse than that, kid," Herzl answered.

The Yids had eked out a precarious existence in the Middle Eastside for as long as anyone could remember.

Ever since the Butcher Shop closed its doors for good generations back, things had all gone downhill.

Plenty of the original gang in the neighborhood had wandered off to the other boroughs. They'd even tried to meld in with the gangs that were around before Nasser came on the scene. Nothing really took.

By the time Herzl came to this part of town to make a go of it, he couldn't really set himself up as a boss like the

17

other bosses. He had a weird status: independent, but always needing to look over his shoulder.

It was a precarious lot. He had to protect the tiny domain and that meant putting up a front of strength so no one could walk all over them.. And he had to pretend he was still small potatoes even as his operation grew, so Nasser's crews would get the idea he wasn't worth the trouble of knocking over.

As usual, the Yids in these parts were a band of losers; wandering, never quite able to fit in wherever they went.

It was embarrassing as all hell.

Zev shifted his view to the photograph on the wall behind Herzl's desk. He noticed a man with expensive spectacles and full beard in a stained butcher's smock. He was looking out from a shop with big cattle carcasses hanging from hooks. He wasn't smiling. But he seemed at home. Really, like he was almost part of his surroundings.

Now Herschel Polanski's son looked at the street in front of the shop and the rustic area. He slowly turned his gaze from the photograph to the scene outside.

The man in the photograph seemed to be looking straight at him.

Zev stared. "That's David himself."

"History is all around us, kid," Herzl interrupted. "The photograph's been in my family for as long as anyone can remember.

"I brought it here from Central Station. Aside from this pipe, it's all I have to remember the old places by. Gruber such made a mess of everything."

Polanski realized Herzl was more like his father than he liked to admit; not in a good way. He'd gotten a look at the quality of Herzl's crew. It was a washout. There were a few tough nuts in there; mostly guys who'd spent a little time in Central Station before the war.

Herzl's crew was pretty much all about the loan-sharking and knock-off goods rackets. They'd been locked out of gun-running, the drug trade, all the lucrative stuff that could buy top talent and real enforcers. You could practically give some switchblades to any fish in the shops and end up

18

with same level of street-fighting prowess. These boys needed to be whipped into shape. And from the sound of it, there wasn't much time to get them ready.

"But I didn't call you in here to discuss old photographs, Polanski."

Herzl looked closely at his new recruit. It was now two weeks since this defeated ghost of a shlammer came calling at the Citadel. The wire-thin short-cropped kid still drew his belt up to the tightest notch on his belt.

But the shlammer had a little toughness to him now. Sinewy. And his eyes saw things. Polanski had lost that haunted look that the other Central Station shtarkes sported.

Herzl decided this one took after his father; he'd been broken down. But he wasn't going to stay that way.

A shlammer like this, even one that would take weeks to grow a decent beard, could be very useful.

"We used to have a nice little operation at the Citadel," Herzl began, blowing smoke rings towards the window. "We made a living. Times are tough, now. And we're going to need to make some changes."

"And I was just getting comfortable," Polanski replied.

"Big Ben was already sour on this neighborhood before your crew showed up," Herzl explained. "He never got much percentage out of the rackets he runs here. Now Nasser is the big macher. He can hit up Big Ben for the rest of the margin.

"That's why our protection money isn't buying us shit. And Nasser's enforcer, Fariq, he's been making trouble for the Citadel's shlameils since before I got here."

Herzl paused to re-light his pipe. "We need more of you Central Station toughs. The losers I found when I first came here were already pretty useless as street hoods. Fariq's shtarkes still wipe the floor with them any chance they get. I got a few good guys. My nephew, Boaz. And Chernik. Some of your pals who came in with you are going to punch above their weight. I see that already. But mostly, our people are lacking in the skills that are most critical for this business."

"Tell me what you need, Herzl."

"If we don't get some guns, all this new blood from Central Station won't matter," Herzl answered. "We're looking at a war in the Middle Eastside. Everyone can see it coming. To tell you the truth, if the Muj gangsters realized just how weak our position was, they would have already moved against us, Big Ben or no Big Ben."

"It's not going to be easy getting guns through Big Ben's goons," Zev noted. "Where do you think we can get 'em?"

"You've got to head up north for a bit," the boss answered.

Zev's eyes narrowed. "Not my first choice, Herzl."

"Where else, then?" Herzl asked, punctuating the remark with another smoke ring. "Besides, you'll be able to open some doors for us. Your father was betrayed, but he was also respected in some quarters. He knew the right people. Try Ivan first."

"Ivan's a two-faced rat bastard," Zev snarled.

"The Upper Eastside is lousy with guns," Herzl replied. "We need as much firepower as we can get and we need it cheap. Our financials aren't exactly healthy. Besides, when he finally moved against Gruber, he saved a lot of Yids. That's just the facts."

Zev hesitated. "Big Ben isn't going to like us going to these people. I've got some other connections I can try."

"Try them, then," Herzl answered. "But go to Ivan first. And fuck Big Ben. The tribute I send him every month goes to his chaneles. He's got no more pull in this neighborhood and everyone knows it. And from what I'm hearing, we're already on borrowed time. So we have to move now."

Zev's right eyebrow perked up. "Hey, you hear that, boss?"

Suddenly, there was shouting outside. Herzl and Polanski looked out the window to see the source of the commotion. "Trouble brewing, kid."

4
WAR POSTPONED

Four Muj shlammers moved in on Boaz. It wasn't looking good for the big Yid.

"Get back in the car," Boaz bellowed. "If you know what's good for you, you meshuger cocksuckers."

Boaz could see in the reflection of the shiny tinted car windows that the rest of the crew outside were not exactly rushing to his defense. Gutless schnooks, most of them. And the ones who could actually back him up, hard men like Chernik and Bibi, were out running rackets.

Bad timing.

Abandoned and despite himself, Boaz' size-fourteen shoes started inching back.

Fariq's men swarmed the fat man. Fariq himself, wearing dark sunglasses with frames so big they made him seem a comic figure, stood just inches from Boaz's beard. "We're here to see Herzl," he snarled. "Go get your boss, you fat fuck."

"Make an appointment if you want to see the macher so bad," Boaz answered. His tone was defiant, though he retreated by inches. "Try next week. Maybe bring flowers."

Fariq pushed his sunglasses forward. He glared into Boaz's beady eyes. Nasser's lieutenant ran his fingers through his oiled-down curly mane and whistled.

"Listen very closely, my chubby friend. I am going to give you one last chance to move your giant ass. Bring your boss to where you're standing right now."

"And I'm telling you, you don't have an appointment, you greasy son of a discounted whore," Boaz replied.

Now he stood his ground and loomed over Fariq like a grumpy colossus.

For a moment, they just stood in the middle of the street.

21

The rest of Herzl's useless crew hid within the walls of the Citadel. A few ancient rifle muzzles pointed out of the windows at the scene in the street. But it was even odds as to whether the shivering shlammers with their fingers on the triggers had even remembered to load their weapons.

From just about any angle, they'd be as likely to shoot down Boaz as the shtarkes who surrounded him.

"Hold him," Fariq commanded. His henchmen grabbed Boaz's arms and struggled to keep the behemoth still.

Fariq withdrew a switchblade from his pocket. He popped the knife.

He was already creasing Boaz's neck by a quarter inch when the front door of the Citadel burst open.

Herzl's face was beet red. There was fury in his eyes. You couldn't tell if it was directed more at the intruders or his useless crew that hung back as one of their own seemed on the verge of getting his throat opened.

Either way, the boss was ready to pop a blood vessel or two.

Polanski was beside him. In contrast to Herzl, the kid was all business. He looked straight through Fariq's hoods with an eerie sort of cool.

Their guns were drawn and they were ready for anything.

At the sight of them, Fariq's henchmen took their hands off Boaz.

"You wanted to see me, you should have made an appointment," Herzl shouted. His eyes were still crazed as he continued to draw a bead on Fariq's head with his shotgun.

"That's what I told him," Boaz answered back. He stepped back to join his reinforcements while wiping the little trail of blood from his throat.

"Go ahead," Polanski suggested in a cold, hollow voice to the nearest of Fariq's shlammers. The thug's clumsy hand was still struggling to grasp the bulge in his breast pocket.

"Do it. Just give me an excuse, muckity-muck."

"Who's the new kid, Herzl?" Fariq shouted. "Your boy's got an attitude.

22

"Salim, put your damn hand where our friends can see it. They don't need to see your drivers' license."

Salim complied. The rest of Fariq's henchmen followed suit.

"You've got some chutzpah, Fariq," Herzl growled. "You're on my turf. Tell me why I shouldn't shoot your balls off right here."

"You kill me, you know you won't live through the night," Fariq answered. He slowly moved his right hand up to rebalance his majestic sunglasses. Somehow, they'd ended up hanging at a forty-five degree angle on his long narrow nose. "Nasser will come down here and throw your people off the pier if you try it."

"I didn't say anything about killing you," Herzl offered. "I just said I was going to relieve you of your nutsack."

He lowered his gun barrel to point at Fariq's crotch. Fariq's eyes went wide. His olive skin turned a pale shade of white.

Just then, another black car started speeding in towards the Citadel from the east end of the street.

Herzl kept his gun trained on Fariq while Zev brought his pistol on the driver.

The car braked and swerved up on to the curb. The driver got out with his hands up, though he didn't look all that flustered. Big Ben's crew was built on this type: solid, unflappable and always a bit mad.

He walked towards the standoff with a casual gait, letting one of his hands drift down momentarily to rebalance his bowler hat.

"Cheers, boys," the messenger exclaimed. "Nice weather you're having down here. Shouldn't you all be cooling off in the shade?"

He had the mid-length wavy hair, bad teeth and cocky demeanor universal to Big Ben's crew. His weird exuberance was distracting enough that all of the shlammers on the street felt a few degrees of fighting spirit sweat out of them.

"What's this, then? Look, chums, come on. Big Ben isn't a fan of these scenes. Put your pistols away."

Herzl's crew complied. But they kept a steady eye trained on Fariq's men.

"We've got a problem, here, Jack," Herzl started. "As you can see, Mr. Fariq has come uninvited to the Citadel Hotel. I'm afraid there's no room at the inn for his type. We're all booked up."

"Hmmm, I see," Jack replied, stroking his chin while keeping his nose upward by a couple of degrees. "Well, you know, Uncle Herzl, that's precisely the problem that I believe Mr. Fariq came here to talk with you about. Frankly, Big Ben was also concerned at the number of guests you've got. There seems to be a bit of an issue with crowding in the Middle Eastside."

"You tell him," Fariq interrupted, trying to egg Jack on. "It's a disgrace. These Yid bastards are stinking up the whole neighborhood. We can smell the Citadel from twenty blocks away.

"This big-nosed fool thinks he's going to start expanding his operation into my side of the street? If Big Ben doesn't take care of this, he's going to see some awful sticky crowd-control measures here."

"Now, now. You swarthy fellows are so damned excitable." Jack's patience with Fariq was wearing thin very quickly. "Perhaps my good news will help calm your nerves."

Both sides now knew something was up. They tapped their feet and rolled their eyes impatiently, knowing Jack was deliberately letting the moment draw out.

Big Ben's messenger smiled a broad grin with his big crooked teeth.

"Times are changing, boys. There's been a significant restructuring of my employer's operations in order to adapt to present business realities. We will be turning over our interests to the locals. That is to say, you fellows."

"About time," Fariq snorted.

"My employer is liquidating his holdings in the Middle Eastside. I'm afraid this includes the generous insurance policies we've provided to both you, Uncle Herzl, and our esteemed colleague, Mr. Fariq."

24

Uncle Herzl grimaced. He knew this moment was a long time coming. He'd even hoped it would happen at some point. But the timing was less than perfect. A lot less.

"Mr. Herzl's organization will retain ownership of the Citadel Hotel and the residences along this side of the street. Mr. Fariq, you will retain ownership of your current holdings conditional on the word of Mr. Nasser's representatives. We expect to have those details finalized shortly."

Fariq's smile turned into a sneer. "Big Ben can't seriously expect me to tolerate this crook's continuing presence in the neighborhood."

"So says the biggest crook on the street," Herzl countered. "We belong on this street, too. And we'll fight for it, Muj. You come near when Big Ben's goons aren't around and you'll see what you get."

Jack was unperturbed. "Big Ben expects you gentlemen to carry on business in a manner consistent with your long-term commercial interests. Violent disruptions are bad for business."

"Not that you bowler hats ever did do that much for us when we were paying you," Herzl grumbled. "Thanks for nothing, Jack."

"Let the man talk," Fariq gloated. "When will you be leaving the neighborhood, then?"

Big Ben's enforcer was already moving back to his car. "Just a little while longer, my friends. Of course, feel free to drop by sometime for a pint if you're ever in Central Station. Big Ben loves an excuse to whet his whistle."

"How long?" Herzl growled.

"Three days," Jack answered, just as he was getting into his vehicle. "You've got three days, Herzl. Tah."

The black cab drove away.

5

BUSINESS TRIP

The subway car was empty except for Herzl's chosen crew and one of Big Ben's shtarkes pretending to read a newspaper way down at the other end. Polanski faced Boaz and Weissman in the gloom of the tunnel's darkness and the train's artificial glow. The train rumbled along towards Central Station.

"What's in the briefcase, Weissman?" Polanski asked.

Weissman did not answer right away. He picked up his wire-rim glasses off his prominent hook nose and cleaned them with a tiny rag. Weissman was dressed in a worn but refined pinstriped suit and scuffed but highly-polished leather shoes. He had a moustache, goatee and bald spot that together with his choice of fashion made him look like a one of those fish head doctors.

He was, of course, Herzl's bagman.

The bagman was a rare breed of gangster. Ordinary fish accountants couldn't be trusted to handle the books for a gang boss. You had to be on the inside. You had to have a good head for numbers. Maybe even have some formal education. And a bagman was the one type of gangster that the big boss wanted to be gutless.

Some corruption was only to be expected, but a bagman who wasn't afraid of his boss could utterly ruin a gang. So they had to love money, but fear the power.

Weissman was a perfect bagman. Herzl had joined up with him early on, recruiting him to negotiate the purchase of the Citadel Hotel and a few adjoining properties. He handled the books for all of Herzl's rackets. And when the big shipments were going in or going out, Weissman personally supervised to make sure the deal went down as it was supposed to. After all, if money or goods went missing, he'd be the first one they'd point fingers at.

26

Weissman looked back at Polanski with a non-committal smile. "Just papers, kid," Weissman said in his scratchy, cigar-smoking voice. "Nothing very interesting."

"Save your breath, kid," Boaz added. "Better you keep your mouth shut until you need use it on Ivan's shlong."

"You're projecting, putz," Polanski replied with his customary cool. "And stop calling me kid. Both of you. Only Herzl gets to call me that."

Boaz shrugged. "Look, that's the only way I figure you're going to get us to see that vampire, Ivan. Your pop was such a success at gang diplomacy he died in a cage. No offense, but if Herzl thinks you've inherited your bub's gift for negotiating, we're sunk."

"Then it's bad news for you," Polanski answered. "If he thought you nudniks were up to the job, he wouldn't have sent me along. Would he? Looks like you're ferkakdeh."

Boaz frowned. "You know, kid, I think you got a real problem."

Polanski shrugged. "Keep at it, fat man." He seemed bored. But Boaz was getting more and more agitated. He thought about taking this skinny runt and snapping his spine over his knee. Was Herzl really that sweet on this kid, already? What the hell did he see in him?

Weissman turned to Boaz. "Gentlemen, I would suggest that we try harder to maintain a low profile. This is not a sightseeing tour."

Boaz sneered back at Weissman. He glared at Polanski.

Polanski just stared back. Boaz couldn't crack him that easy.

He still looked frail. The kid was still just 140 pounds on a nearly six-foot frame. His cheeks were sunken. The suit he'd borrowed was everywhere too big on him.

But Polanski had no fear. No anger, either.

He knew why Boaz was annoyed with him. Herzl had taken an interest in Zev. Over the past week, he'd spent more and more time with him than with his old lieutenant.

In the zero-sum game of gang politics, Boaz's place in Herzl's hierarchy was starting to fall. The loyal shlammer resented being usurped by an outsider.

27

Maybe Boaz was right. Polanski carried the wretched stench of cataclysmic failure through his bloodline. Gangs were not a perfect meritocracy. There was always a bit of nepotism built in. And the sins of the father could carry down to the son.

For Boaz, getting rescued in front of the Citadel Hotel by Herzl and Polanski was intolerable. He was still pissed at the rest of the deadbeats at the Citadel who had failed to get his back. But it was almost worse that this kid was the one everyone had their eye on now.

Weissman was correct that this journey would be no sightseeing tour. But when the subway train emerged into the light of the first stop at Central Station, the sight beyond the rails was something else.

Particularly for Zev, it was a shock. He'd seen this place back in the glory days when the Polanski gang still strutted along its side streets (and kept away from the main thoroughfares where the rival gangs held sway). Seeing the ruined and blighted cityscape again brought on an awesome wellspring of dark emotions.

There was some sadness there. But another part of him felt like this place just looked like it should. Like it deserved to be.

Central Station was in ruins.

The streets to the north and south were still marked by car-sized potholes and debris. Every building that still stood had the scars of Gruber's bloody turf war.

Many buildings had collapsed from fires and relentless bombing.

The conquerors had moved quickly into the abandoned warehouses and utility buildings. There were even some new businesses there. The fish that remained were as industrious as always.

With Gruber's soldiers exterminated, Ivan was cashing in. He'd put all of Gruber's molls to work for him. But he wasn't even doing it for the money. Mostly, he set it up just to service his own enforcers pro bono off the silk-stocking spoils of war.

28

All of the gangs were making huge profits from the trade in guns and drugs. In the midst of this utter wreck, there could be no better market conditions for the underworld economy. The fish were biting.

A few more stops along the subway route, the place actually became more depressing. The place was all black ash and gray dust. Cracked cement and crushed masonry. Broken bones gnawed by rats in the back alleys.

These were the areas where Gruber and Ivan's forces had gone at it. They'd traded advantage on a fluid battlefield. The only constant was corpses in the gutters.

But there was still a kind of life in this part of the City. You couldn't set up shop, here. But no part of this borough was going to stay empty for long. Scorched earth was still turf.

Ivan's henchmen perched on rooftops and stood on street corners. They were always on alert. Were they really worried about Washington or the old crews from Central Station causing trouble? Probably not, even though Ivan grumbled constantly about them. The other bosses were in no mood to start a new war.

These days, Ivan's most trusted shtarkes kept themselves busy by keeping tabs on everyone else in the organization. They cannibalized their own shtarkers for the slightest show of disloyalty to Ivan, real or imagined.

There was a freezer unit at the Lubyanka meat-packing plant near Ivan's headquarters. Some said it was packed wall to wall with gonifs and trigger-men deemed insufficiently stooge-like towards their boss. Gruber was gone, but there was an awfully good chance that Ivan was going to one-up the scale of his thuggishness some day.

Herzl's crew were getting closer to their final destination. They caught some of Ivan's gunmen staring in at them through the windows. Their eyes were like cold steel. They stood straight like real soldiers. Each of them held an automatic rifle at the ready.

Weissman leaned in towards Zev. "Our boss has great faith in your connections, kid. I'm not knocking you, but I hope for our sake he's made the right call."

"We'll know pretty soon," Polanski answered. "If he's wrong, it's been nice knowing you Yids."

The train came to a full stop. The trio exited. They were immediately intercepted by two men with utilitarian crew hats and bomber jackets. They swung their AK-47s around to a threatening angle.

"A little far from the Middle Eastside, comrades," the slightly less stone-faced hood began, addressing them with a voice like frozen gravel. "Ivan doesn't like strangers poking around here. Who's this, with you? You from Central Station?"

"Can't put one past you Eastsiders," Polanski replied. "Zev Polanski from Central Station at your service. My friends form the Middle Eastside are enjoying the scenery."

At the name, the twin towering henchmen both seemed to be trying to place it, their foreheads, crossing ever so slightly with a hint of modest brainpower. "I got it," the second one said, snapping his fingers. "Herschel Polanski's kid."

"No joke," the first one replied. "Huh. And what is this kid with you beards, then? What's your business?"

"We're here to see Ivan," Zev answered, surprising the two guards by taking charge. He surprised his companions as well. But in this place, he wasn't "the kid". He was a gangster with full rank as an enforcer.

"We've got a business proposition. Take us to him."

"This kid!" Weissman interjected. "No tact."

"Leave him to us, kamarads," Boaz added, cracking his knuckles.

"You idiots better come with us," the first of Ivan's shtarkes decided. "Ivan can decide what to do with you."

"Probably toss the lot of them in the freezer," the second shtarke added. "With the meat hooks still in them."

Ivan's hoods armed-to-the-teeth hoods brought Herzl's crew into the heart of the Upper Eastside.

This street had never seen the house-to-house urban warfare that had occurred just a few blocks away. But the area looked just as bleak for that. The store fronts were mostly boarded-up. Shadowy streets led to darker alleys. Only a few cars with tinted windows and bullet-proof plating made their way along these gray roads. Cigarette smoking guards stopped

30

chaneles to actually check their papers, not just try to cop a feel.

They came to Ivan's fortress, known throughout the city as the Cathedral.

At one time it was one of those classic looking stone churches. Now it was topped with a simple star in place of a cross. The exterior had undergone an extensive renovation in keeping with the habit of all City bosses, reinforcing the walls, installing bars on the windows and gun sights at the corners. The black walls sucked in all light. It was like a black hole where no warmth or illumination could ever escape.

It was a cold place. It was a place even gangsters felt uneasy if they had no business there.

At the main entrance, three more guards loitered. Their AK-47s were slung over their shoulder. More guards stood on rooftops or in the windows of the buildings across the street, their locations given away by the red glow from their cigarettes.

The visitors had rarely seen so much firepower on open display. Zev could have sworn he spotted a man with a missile launcher as a silhouette on the roof of the Cathedral. Ivan was manufacturing all kinds of crazy toys.

"Who's this, Zhukov?" one of the guards at the front entrance asked, looking decidedly unhappy at the prospect of dealing with outsiders. "You might have saved yourself the trip and just shot them."

"It was tempting," the first shtarke admitted. "But the skinny one is Herschel Polanski's kid."

"That's interesting."

"Thought it might be worth the boss' time. They say they've got some kind of business."

"Oh yeah? Have they got any cash on them?"

Weissman shrugged. "If it's alright with you gentlemen, I would prefer we discussed it with your employer directly. We're in a bit of a hurry."

"What's in the briefcase, wise guy?" The senior henchman among them asked.

Weissman handed it to them. "It's not locked."

31

They opened the briefcase and looked through the mass of unsorted and dog-eared papers that seemed like a testament to disorganization. "What's this rubbish?" the guard asked.

Weissman smiled. "Contracts. Leases. Herzl's taxes. Receipts from the every entertainment expense I've had in the last decade. Sorry for the mess, fellows."

"I thought you actually went to business school, Weissman," Boaz gasped. He slapped the back of his own neck. "You putz. Why the hell does Herzl put up with you?"

Weissman was allowed to pack up his briefcase under the watchful eyes of the guards. "Now, Boaz. There's more to business than paperwork. I've got it all up here," he said, pointing to his rather angular cranium.

"Putz," Boaz answered with a sneer.

"Are we going to see Ivan or not?" Zev asked the senior guard. "I can't stand outside with these numbskulls much longer."

The guard who went inside returned. "Ivan wants to see the kid alone. You bozos can wait on the sidewalk here."

"That's no good," Boaz protested. "It's all or none, comrade."

"Save it, fat man," the guard replied. "I wasn't giving any options. Comrade Polanski, get inside. The boss awaits."

Past the façade of the Cathedral, the interior was all gray walls and hard angles. Zev was ushered past what looked like prison cells. A little further in, past a creaky staircase and more cigarette-smoke filled halls populated with automatic-toting kamarads, they finally came to a heavy black metal door.

Two of the thickest, most brutal shlammers Zev had ever seen, bristling with armament, stood on either side of the door. Zev's escort nodded at them. The one on the right rapped his knuckles on the formidable entrance.

"Herschel Polanski's kid is here to see you, boss," the guard spoke into an intercom.

The door buzzed and opened a few inches inward. "Go straight in, kid," the guard whispered. "Ivan's in a rare mood."

Zev entered Ivan's office. The bald, powerful-looking patriarch of the Upper Eastside gang was obscured by shadow. A single light on the ceiling failed to illuminate the space around the boss. It was as though his presence sucked the light like a black hole.

The air in the room was stale. Polanski noticed the walls were decorated with rifles and machine-guns. They were interspersed with faded pictures and maps of the gray and desolate tenements of Ivan's territory. The boss had pretty much defined himself by this war just fought. Maybe a war to come, too.

Ivan stayed in his chair. He was a hulking frame in a plain-looking shirt and tie. When he spoke, it was like a rumble from a volcano.

"Come closer, kid," Ivan began. "Comrade Polanski's son. This is a surprise."

"Us Yids are turning up in the most unlikely places."

Just the barest trace of a smile appeared on Ivan's face. Or maybe Polanski had imagined it. "So you made it out of Central Station. No bear cage for you, like your father? So how come you're not dead?"

"Lucky, I guess," Zev answered.

"Lucky?" Ivan offered a wheezy, cigar-smoking kind of laugh. "Luck had nothing to do with what happened to your people. Never has. All of you bloodsuckers from the Middle Eastside are the same. The Polanski's, the Herzl's, the Lansky's, the Levi's... It seems your people have a death wish."

"You think so? I'd say we're just trying to survive, like everyone else," Zev answered.

"I think that's your problem," Ivan countered. "Just trying to survive doesn't cut it, comrade Polanski. While your people were scraping by through the tough years, us real gangsters were building up. Your father was a distraction. A nuisance."

Polanski frowned. But he kept his mouth shut.

"Your father was all about scraping off the crumbs just enough for his crew to keep fed, without pissing off bosses like me... and none of it mattered. In this City, friends don't give you turf. Protection money only lasts so long before the guy

33

you're paying gets greedy. That racket's for fish, not real gangsters."

Ivan was warming to the topic. "Survival? That's a loser's dream. You want to get along in this place, you've got to dominate."

"Then us Yids are all out of luck," Polanski said with a shrug. "Surviving's all we've got."

Ivan nodded his head just a tiny bit. The faintest hint of a smile edged its way into the corner of his mouth, but only for the briefest of moments. "So you've come here for a business deal. You need guns."

"What else?" Polanski answered.

There was silence in the room for a moment. Ivan seemed to be studying Zev's face for something, perhaps some resemblance to his father.

Zev wasn't sure. Still, he showed no sign of any disquiet. He kept his cool.

"I remember when your father was just starting out. Even at the beginning, the odds were dead set against him and he knew it. He had to know it."

"I thought we were going to talk business," Polanski said. Polanski tried to see Ivan's face, but now it was lost in silhouette.

Ivan ignored him. "I don't think that Yid even wanted much to be a boss. The Polanski crew didn't much want to be gangsters, either. You know that. The other gangs of Central Station wouldn't have them. And the territories were already pretty well carved up. So what can you do, comrade? Man's got to eat."

Zev nodded. He wasn't sure where Ivan was headed with this history lesson. But he knew better than to interrupt the boss of the Upper Eastside. He waited for an opening.

"I made your father an offer once. Real protection. Permanent. And Comrade Polanski turned me down." Ivan was glaring at Zev now. His face got darker with each passing moment.

Polanski shrugged. "I don't know what kind of terms you offered my father. I don't know what went on between you. But that's in the past. And I'm not here representing myself.

34

Herzl is the one you're dealing with. Forget the name, Polanski. Herzl is the name of the man who wants to buy your guns."

Ivan nodded. "You're right about one thing, kid. You've got no idea."

Polanski frowned. Ivan was playing with him. "Look, Ivan, this is a pure business opportunity. That's all it is. You've got guns. Herzl's got cash. We're all gangsters. It's simple. It's business."

Ivan gazed at a Bren machine gun he'd mounted on the wall. "Business," he grunted. "You're right. It is about business, Comrade Polanski. But our business isn't about making money. It's about who has the guns."

"We've got the money," Polanski said. "We'll pay. And don't try to tell me you haven't got the merchandise. Your turf's swimming with guns."

Ivan shook his head. "We do things differently here in the Upper Eastside, Comrade Polanski. Supply and demand? Cash flow and profits? None of that matters.

"I would happily give away ten trucks filled to the roof with more guns and ammo than you've ever seen, to the right shlammers. I'd give it away. But there's no point with you."

Ivan stroked the barrel of his machine gun mounted on his wall like he was petting a cat. "You and the rest of you Yids are losers, Polanski. You've never won a fight. And it's just a matter of time before Nasser's boys roll into Uncle Herzl's little hotel and slit all of your throats. And those are the shlammers I want to do business with.

"Soon, the last of your people will finally be buried in a big ditch or sleeping at the bottom of the harbor. When that happens, you know what I'm going to do?"

"No," Polanski said, his eyes narrowed to slits. "You tell me."

"I'll make a phone call to the people who did it. I'll tell him, 'Congratulations on wiping out the last of those filthy cockroaches'. Now get the fuck out my office before I save Nasser the trouble of a bullet."

6
MONEY AND POWER

The gleaming glass elevator kept going up and up. None of the tired and sweaty crew had ever experienced anything like it.

Boaz discovered for the first time in his life that he was afraid of heights. He hugged the wall while keeping his eyes perfectly shut. It didn't help him much. Weissman and Polanski meanwhile gazed open-mouthed on the incredible skyline that grew before them.

It wasn't just the tall buildings that rose like mutant mushrooms from the well-trafficked streets below. There was green in this concrete jungle. Washington's territory was full of parks and open lawns manicured by fish and old shlammers put out to pasture.

Further away, you could see tenements and houses where it was rumored Washington had developed some sort of economy that did not rely on criminal enterprise. The fish were making Washington richer than any gangster who had ever lived.

Who knew how they could make a buck? But they did. Hand over fist. This part of the City was a real land of opportunity for a mensch on the make.

Finally, they reached the ninety-eighth floor of the Chrysler building. The place was named for one of Washington's favored predecessors. Incredibly, there were still another ten floors and a rooftop off limits to visitors.

The crew stepped into a shiny marble lobby with floor to ceiling windows showing off the City as far as the edge of the ruins of Central Station to the east.

"Herzl wasn't kidding about your name opening doors, kid," Weissman snickered, wiping his spectacles with a handkerchief. "This is some view. These Upper Westsiders know how to live."

He let out a whistle as his eyes fell on the buxom blonde lady at the black mahogany desk. She was a knockout. The astonished Middle Eastsiders looked from one incredible sight to the next. Washington recruited only the finest chaneles.

But Boaz was still in an awful mood from the four-minute ascent. "We're in, alright. But we didn't come here to sightsee."

"We'll see if Washington wants to do business then," Weissman said with a shrug. "Kid, you're up."

Their wiry companion introduced himself to the blonde. "Zev Polanski. I'm here to see Washington."

"The boss is expecting you," she answered in a sultry voice that had left countless men salivating. Money and power. This is what it all came down to.

"You can all go in."

There were no further security checks. They'd all been screened with X-rays and metal detectors when they came into the ground-floor lobby. From there on in, Washington's security measures were invisible; though the trio had no doubt that at the first sign of trouble, they'd all end up taking 98-floor swan dives to the concrete pavement.

Washington's office was just as bright and opulent as the lobby. Washington was standing by the window admiring another majestic view of the City. His City.

His pin-striped suit and brilliant black loafers probably cost more than a brand-new car. And he wore it well. His silver-white hair was slicked back underneath a flamboyant top-hat that somehow didn't look out of place indoors. A distinctive white goatee that would have looked ridiculous on the other men in the room likewise marked Washington out as royalty.

He was like a thoroughly modern Nebuchadnezzar.

Boss of bosses. King of the gangsters.

Washington turned to face them.

"Can I offer you boys something to drink?" His voice had a sort of rustic hospitality mixed with the confidence of a corporate shark.

They quickly dispatched with polite introductions. He pointed to an open bar stocked with the finest aged malts. "Please do make yourself at home."

"Don't mind if I do," Weissman obliged, speeding to the bar and pouring himself two fingers of whiskey. Boaz grimaced at Weissman's greedy quickness. He stood firmly in place.

"Some digs you've got here, Washington," Polanski said, putting his hand out. "If I really made myself at home, I'd never want to leave."

Washington nodded. "Many of your people are already here. Mostly the fish. But some of the Polanski crew came over since the war in Central Station."

"That's good news," Polanski said. "Wish I had time to catch up with them. I hope they're fitting in."

"Your kind have made themselves useful since I first set up operations. Since before this was Big Ben's turf and we were at each other's throats. We are grateful for their profitable contribution to our enterprise."

"That's very kind. Uncle Herzl and my father always looked up to you, Washington. It's too bad you're such a long ride away."

"The feeling is mutual," Washington added. "But enough of this mutual admiration society pleasantries. You've come to do business. And let's face it, my business is business. But I regret to tell you that you may have come in vain."

Polanski's ears pricked up at that. "I thought this was a place where money talks. We're ready to deal. Herzl's money's good."

"It's all a bit complicated," Washington apologized. "But tell me, why did you go to Ivan before you came to see me?"

Polanski shrugged. "I was dead-set against going to him at all. But to be totally straight with you, Herzl figured we might get more bang for our buck on the Upper Eastside. That rat's got more guns than shtarkes to shoot 'em. It was nothing against you."

Washington nodded. "Herzl was always good with the business side of things. Hell, most of your guys are. But as much as I'm a businessman, I am at heart a gangster. I don't make my money by selling kitchen widgets to the masses. We make our profit over the dead bodies of our enemies lying in the gutter."

"Funny, Ivan said pretty much the same thing," Polanski said. "But I don't see a problem."

"Fair enough," Washington answered with a disarming smile. "Look, let me explain. See Boaz Livni, here," he said, pointing to the hulking brute. Boaz was starting incredulously at an abstract painting he could make heads nor tails of. At the mention of his name, he turned to the boss of bosses.

"So you've heard of me?" Boaz answered incredulously. "What have you got, a file on every shlammer from here to David's Butcher Shop?"

"I pay my people to do their homework," Washington said. "See, Boaz attracted some attention two seasons ago when he single-handedly pulverized two of Fariq al Barghouti's men in an alley. You permanently paralyzed the third member of that crew. And this wasn't the first time you'd displayed a singular talent. You know how to brutalize your enemies. And you've earned quite the reputation in your neck of the woods."

"They attacked me first," Boaz answered, not quite sure why he felt compelled to excuse his conduct.

"Precisely," Washington continued. "You're a cagey fighter. And a loyal one as well. Boaz here has been with Herzl almost since the beginning, running his rackets, keeping order in the neighborhood with a monopoly of violence. You've got a proven track record as an enforcer."

Boas wasn't all that used to positive reinforcement. He remained silent as he waited for the other shoe to drop.

"And Zev, here... Do you mind if I call you Zev? No disrespect, but you've barely got stubble on your face. I just find it strange to call you Mr. Polanski. That's what I called your father back in the day."

Polanski nodded. He still wasn't sure where Washington was going. But it wasn't looking good.

"I know what it took for you to survive Central Station. I've read the field reports. Maybe you can't grow a decent beard like your Yid brothers just yet. But kid, I'd wager you're one of the toughest, most cold-blooded bastards who's ever stood in this office. And I respect the hell out of that."

"So tell me again why we can't do business," Polanski interrupted.

Washington pointed at Weissman. "There's your problem, right there."

"Just a minute, sir," Weissman retorted with a twisted look, glaring through his thick spectacles. "What's the problem you have with me? I've read a book? I can do long division without breaking a sweat?"

"In a manner of speaking, yes," Washington replied. "Don't get me wrong, sir. I can appreciate a man with brains; a fellow who can run the numbers. I've got seven bagmen who do what you do. I'm sure I could put a man like you into any one of my smuggling operations and improve efficiency by half."

"Then what precisely is the problem, Mr. Washington?"

"In the next couple of days, your people won't have enough people like Zev and Mr. Livni. Herzl's got too many smart men who can't fight worth a damn.

"Let's not beat around the bush. You Yids are just not a good long-term investment for me. By doing a deal with you today, I'm just going to piss off your neighbors. More important, I have to worry about our mutual friend in the Upper Eastside having a bad hangover from all of that vodka he drowns himself in. He may just use my involvement as a pretext to make a move in Central Station."

Polanski's eyes narrowed. "You've got more than enough guns and enforcers to mop the floor with Ivan in my old neighborhood. You're not really afraid of fighting."

"I fear no one," Washington said. "But Ivan and me will go to war at a time of my own choosing. I will not be drawn into that fight now. Not by you. It's bad business."

"So we get nothing?" Zev snarled. His cool was gone. Now he was pissed. "You're going to let those fuckers slit our throats? Damn you, Washington. You're worse than Ivan. At least he's consistent about being an asshole."

Their host withdrew slightly, surprised at the sudden change in Polanski's eyes. Already, there were two huge

40

security men at the door to his office. Their hands grasped at the holsters in their jackets.

But Washington waved them off.

"Maybe you're right, you spoiled rich bastard," Polanski thundered while his companions crept backward. He suddenly seemed to have grown a foot, his muscles steeled like a cobra ready to strike. "This isn't just about business. I've waded through buckets of blood. You say you've read some field reports. But you don't know what it was like. It's been ages since you had to kill a man by your own hand. You've forgotten what it's like. I will not let my people go down like they did in Central Station. We will fight... with or without your guns. We will do whatever we have to do to win."

Now he just stood there. His chest rumbled. His face was red. He was still furious. The security men watched for a signal from the Boss of Bosses.

"You've got guts, Mr. Polanski," Washington started. "There's no question. Maybe I had you pegged wrong before. You're different from your father. You have gotten my attention."

Washington went to his ancient, brilliantly-polished antique desk and opened a drawer. He withdrew a card from a small box and presented it to Polanski.

"I cannot help you, Mr. Polanski. "But I may know someone who can. Go to the address on this card. I make no promises about this man's reliability. But I don't see that you have many other options."

Polanski nodded, a little calmed but not yet serene. "He'll have the merchandise, then?"

"I make no promised of this man. And you didn't get his address from me. But if he helps you... and if you and your friends are still breathing after this all blows over, then there will be opportunities for us to work together."

"So that's it, thenn?"

"Just get through this and we can talk. Good luck. And God bless."

As the trio left, Washington watched them hurry into the elevator, heading out on a mission with little to no chance of success.

He had to admire the kid's tenacity.

The security guards vanished as the buxom blonde receptionist came to the room. Like magic, the glass of the office became a reflective mirror, allowing them total privacy. "Ready for me to suck your cock, sir?"

Washington nodded. "It's good to be the boss."

7

CHASING MEMORIES

"So, four-eyes? Any idea how we get to this dealer without bringing Ivan's shtarkes down on our heads?" Boaz asked Weissman. "Washington's sending us on a wild goose chase if you ask me."

"The address is right on the border zone," Weissman acknowledged. He watched as the glamorous towers of the Washington's domain faded into the distance and an plain of dead space opened up on the way to the ruins of Central Station. "The guards will be suspicious at us trying to get back in. Especially considering their boss was about ready to throw us on to meat hooks when we got the boot."

"We get the guns from this meshuga arms dealer or we're all finished," Polanski said, wakening briefly from an uncharacteristic calm as he watched the City moving. "So we die here or we die there."

"What's got you so cheerful, kid?" Boaz retorted. "Thinking of the good old days back in Central Station?"

As a matter of fact, he was.

When he'd shouted at Washington, a slew of dark memories bubbled to the surface.

He remembered the smell of blood and shit and gangrene down in the sewers. The hunger that pulled like a knotted cord in his gut. The gurgles of men and women dying from ulcerous gunshot wounds. Infected rat bites. Typhus. The despair.

Tough, brass-knuckles Yid gangsters transformed into skin-and-bones ghosts. They clawed and connived for rotten scraps of food. Polanski could still see their bloody mouths. He could hear their phlegm-choked lungs. He remembered keeping a death-grip on his rust-stained blade, just in case one of his ravenous colleagues felt inspired to make a meal out of him, or Gruber's storm troopers finally found their dank hiding place.

He remembered the sound of the barrage and the fire that licked the frame of the hidden entrance and sucked the air out of their stinking nook. And the terror in the eyes of the last survivors.

And briefly, just as they approached the last station before the border, he thought of her: Justine.

Her face flashed through his brain. Flawless skin and ruby lipstick. Dirty blonde hair. Blue eyes the color of the sky on an early winter morning.

She was older than him. And her body had fully matured. Firm breasts. Hips that invited all kinds of debauchery. Not beautiful. But pretty. Striking. She looked at you with a stare that said she could slit your throat or fuck you – and you wouldn't know which until it happened.

And suddenly, she wasn't just a vision from his memory. He couldn't tell if seeing her had sparked the flashbacks or if his half-remembered dreams had somehow conjured her into reality.

But it was her.

She was there, running down a ruined street pursued by two brawny shlammers in gray overcoats with automatic rifles. They weren't shooting though. They dodged over debris and ran like salivating dogs as Justine tried in vain to put distance between them.

For Polanski, the moment seemed much longer. But in the instant he saw her, he made for the emergency exit of the train connecting carriages.

Boaz and Weissman thought their companion had gone nuts. Before they could react, they saw him yank the train door open and jump on to the embankment on the north side of the tracks.

Polanski rolled down the embankment. He cut his head and legs on little shards of masonry. He somewhat recovered his balance almost at the bottom. He jumped down and broke into a run, miraculously avoiding a sprained ankle or worse. His legs pumped with adrenaline as he scooted past burnt-out cars and boarded-up windows.

He got to the end of the street.

Which way had they gone? A woman's scream eerily cut short drew him to the right.

Now he approached stealthily, keeping low and to the shadows of the last bits of sunlight.

"Now you're going to get it, bitch," Polanski heard a rough voice sputter, lusty and merciless.

"Hold her down, damn it!"

Polanski spied them from outside the old brick building where the front lobby door swung gently, inviting him in. He could make out the two giants inside. One held Justine's head down. Her face was shoved against the filthy wooden boards of a broken floor. The other was frantically unbuttoning his pants in anticipation.

Polanski drew his knife from his sleeve and stalked into the room.

Before the accomplice knew what was happening, his throat was ripped out. The big lug sank to the floor.

The randy titan at the other end tackled Polanski but lost his grip as his undone trousers tripped him up.

The momentum still slammed Polanski against the wall of the entrance. His head rang and he dropped like a shot.

The next thing Polanski knew, the Upper Eastside shtarke was pulling him up. The giant thug slammed his ham of a fist into Polanski's face. It felt like he'd just run face-first into a concrete wall.

The fist came down again. Blood streaked from Polanski's mouth. A tooth bounced off the doorway.

Then the bruiser let go and Polanski was falling against the wall. He collapsed into a heap. His head was still ringing. The room was spinning.

But at the far end of the room in the shadows, he could make out Boaz grappling with the brute. A guttural choking sound carried through the room.

And then it stopped.

"He's dead, Boaz," Weissman concluded. "I think your strangling technique's improved. I'll have to get Uncle Herzl to give you a little extra this month."

Boaz let the hulk drop to the floor.

His opponent certainly had expired. But the big Yid still kicked him in the ribs for good measure, snapping two of them.

Weissman slapped Polanski out of his stunned state. "Zev, I hope this young lady's worth it. Ivan's boys are going to be on top of us like a bag of snakes."

Justine sat in the middle of the room with her arms curled round her legs. She was still in a state of shock.

But at the mention of Zev's name, she seemed to wake up from it.

"Zev? Zev Polanski? Is that really you?"

Polanski pulled himself to his feet, nearly falling back down before Weissman held him up. "It's me. I saw you from the train."

"But how did you get out from Central Station?"

"Does it matter?" he answered, finally breaking into a smile. "It's good to see you, Justine."

"Sorry to interrupt this happy reunion, but can someone tell me what's going on here?" Boaz interjected. "I'd like to know why I had to strangle that poor sap in the corner. And why this other one is leaking into the floor. And why we're all probably going to be dead in the next twenty minutes."

"Justine is an old friend," Polanski explained. "When Gruber took over in Central Station, she helped some of us stay out of sight."

"For all the good it did you," Justine replied, drilling a hole into the floor with her stare.

"You bought us time," Polanski answered, coming over and putting his hand on her shoulder. "Some of them made it out because of you."

"So what are you doing here in Central Station?" Weissman asked. "Why didn't you come to the Middle Eastside with the others?"

"Justine was one of Gruber's molls," Polanski said. "This is where she lives."

Boaz whistled. "Nice company you keep, Polanski. Don't that beat all."

"It's not my territory anymore," Justine answered. "Ivan's pigs are crawling all over this place. Except for the pockets where Washington's got his claws in, it's just turning into an extension of the Upper Eastside. Every snatch they can get their hands on ends up in the brothels. And he just gives the worst thugs the run of the house. It's no way for a lady to make a living."

"Why don't you try to get out?" Weissman asked. "Go to the other side."

"My place is here," she replied. "I've got good work, too. I work for a gun-runner in the lower tenements."

Weissman's ears pricked up at that. "That's funny. We were just on our way to the lower tenements. And we were actually wondering how we were going to get past the border to get into there. It's going to be particularly dicey when these two fellows get reported missing."

"I can take you there," Justine said, having reclaimed her typical strong-willed nature. "The train's no good. You're bound to get stopped by Ivan's men. I know another way."

Polanski nodded. "You lead, then."

"How do we know we can trust her?" Boaz said, suddenly suspicious. "Just because she helped you before doesn't mean she's not going to give us up now. Her being one of Gruber's old molls isn't such a great reference. Know what I mean?"

"You just saved me," Justine explained with cold patience. "I may have been with Gruber's crew once. But I'm not completely inhuman."

"Let's move," Polanski said, keeping a wary eye on Boaz.

Weissman gave Boaz a gentle punch in the arm. "It's dark out there, my friend. And without a guide who knows these streets, we're sure to get snatched. A little faith in Polanski's lady, yes?"

Boaz grunted his assent. The crew went back into the darkening street. With any luck, they'd get away before Ivan's enforcer's came calling.

8

THE ARMS DEALER

Justine cursed her clumsy companions under her breath. They stumbled over broken blocks and vehicle parts that littered the street. Polanski moved with practiced stealth learned from dodging Gruber's forces for months on end. But Weissman and Boaz bumped up against the concrete and rusted lids that scattered and clanked in the dark.

At any moment, a burst from a submachine gun could signal their end.

"There's not a single patch of ground here without some piece of ground stabbing at me," Boaz whispered. "I nearly broke my leg off at the knee back there."

"Quiet, Yids," Polanski warned. "We don't need to make it easy for these shtarkes to end our little working trip."

"We're almost there," Justine reassured them. "Stay close to this wall. When you get to the end, wait until you see my signal, then go towards it." She scampered ahead despite the darkness. Soon, she was out of earshot.

"How can she find her way?" Weissman asked Polanski. "She must be half-cat."

Polanski shrugged. "Something like that. But like someone else said, I don't see like we have other options."

"You're right about that, kid."

About twenty yards away and to the left, a flashlight shone three times at them from a crack in the wall. They made their way to a cracked wall with a boarded up section.

Justine creaked opened a disguised entrance an arm's length and they trundled in. The crew was only slightly relieved at making it off the street and into a dark and dusty hallway barely wide enough for Boaz to walk through sideways.

An utterly out-of-place thick wooden door with a brass frame stood at the end. A sliding metal pane opened and bloodshot eyes with furry eyebrows glared at Justine in the lead.

"We're closed for business," he warned with an accent none of the visitors could quite place. "Justine, I don't know who your friends are, but..."

"Let us in, Tito," Justine interrupted. "They're friends."

"You don't have any friends," the voice came back, still suspicious but slightly softened.

"Zev Polanski and his Yid crew," Justine answered.

"You bring me Yids? Like I need the trouble."

"Open the door or we're done, Tito."

The sound of big lock turning over came a few seconds later -- followed by a series of countless other locks of all kinds. Finally, the door swung back.

"Get in here," Tito commanded, standing back enough for the rest of them to enter what looked like an abandoned depot office. "Hell of a time to drop in for a party, friends."

"This is a business call," Zev announced. "We have a friend on the Upper Westside who says you're in the arms business."

"Then you'll have to thank your friend for the referral," Tito said, lighting up a cheap cigarette. "Always glad to have new customers. It would be nice if you kept more regular hours. But this is the type of business we're in, eh?"

He was a balding, middle-aged man with crooked teeth and a cheap brown suit and an ancient cream-colored shirt. His fingertips were stained yellow with nicotine and he had a stoop that made him look about twenty years older than his real age.

On closer inspection in the better light of the office, Tito seemed a little surprised to see the skinny kid talking for the group. "So you've got friends in high places, then. They can't get you what you need?"

"It's complicated," Weissman interjected. "Do you have the merchandise?"

Tito nodded. "Not on the premises," he clarified. "But my suppliers are good. There's enough black-market arms hidden around Central Station to start a new war. Any quantities you need."

"How soon can you get them?" Zev

"Two days," Tito said. "Maybe four."

Boaz shook his head. "This is cutting it too close. Big Ben's shtarkes will be thick on the ground on all the routes into the Middle Eastside just before they pull out. And they'll be looking for us. We have to close this deal tonight."

"Wait, wait," Tito interrupted. "You need these shipped into the Middle Eastside? You can't take them back with you?"

The three Yids nodded in unison. They had to get back.

"As you say, you'll never get it through Big Ben's blockade. And there's just no way I can get you the guns tonight."

"You have a proposal, then?" Weissman asked.

"I can make all the arrangements and get them to the Middle Eastside, past Big Ben. I'll have to do it myself."

"Good luck with that," Boaz interjected. "Looks like we're ferkakdeh."

Justine had listened careful, but now she joined in. "Tito can get through. He's been working both sides for years. He's got connections."

Tito shrugged. "I'm not in the habit of bragging, but the lady speaks the truth. Most people think this street is Ivan's turf. But I make a living here. The locals want a boss they can trust. I can get past Ivan's gangsters. And I can grease some palms from Big Ben's crew if I need to."

Weissman nodded tentatively.

"Of course, I'll need you to cover these kinds of expenses. And since it seems like you have to leave in a hurry, I'll need payment in advance."

"Get serious," Boaz growled. "We're not going to pay you before we see the goods. Besides, it doesn't help us if we get the guns in a week. Herzl's going to need them sooner than that."

"I don't see that you Yids have a choice," Tito answered without skipping a beat. "I'm a businessman, not a miracle worker. You don't want to do business, fine. I have other customers who aren't so demanding."

Zev looked Tito straight in the eyes. "We'll need some kind of guarantees."

Tito shook his head. "There are none. I'm not selling mattresses here, friends. But if you have the cash, I will get your guns. This is my business. And I live or die on my reputation."

Zev looked back at Justine, then the suspicious faces of his companions, then back at Tito. His eyes were cold like a snake's. "You screw us and I'll come back here myself and slit your throat."

"In that case, you don't need my guarantee. Though I appreciate your enthusiasm. Now, are you ready to deal?"

Zev nodded. He looked at his companions.

Weissman put his creaky grease-stained briefcase on the desk and opened it up. Next, he popped open a secret compartment. A fistful of diamonds poured onto the granite table in front of them.

"Herzl's life savings," Weissman said. Everyone around the table admired the shiny treasures. "Now, let's get down to brass tacks. I want to see makes and models and a price list. And samples, too."

"As you wish," Tito said. "Let's do business, then."

9
GOOD RIDDANCE

The early morning light shone in through cracks in the boarded-up windows. Zev woke next to Justine. They were both still wearing their clothes from the previous day. The harsh contours of the Paleolithic fabric sofa were etched into their backs.

They'd collapsed there sometime around three 'o' clock in the morning. The negotiations had gone long. And there was still some catching up to do.

She woke at the same time, rubbing her eyes and yawning widely. "Ouch, my back." She grimaced as she tried to get to her feet.

Polanski's right foot was asleep from getting caught in a nook. He stood up and felt the tingling come, little needles in his toes.

He shook it off, looking around. Boaz and Weissman were still out cold.

"Let's go outside," Justine whispered.

"I thought it wasn't safe out there."

"Just come with me," she insisted. They went down a different hall, opened up a metal door with a mesh grate on top of it and emerged into a tiny courtyard filled with piles of junk. It was enclosed on four sides by blank brick walls.

"I didn't think I'd see you again," Justine said, still stretching to get rid of a pain in her neck.

"I didn't think I'd be coming back here," Polanski answered. "At least not so soon. So what are you going to do?"

"I'll survive," she said with a shrug. "Like I always have. I'll dodge Ivan's shlammers. I'll keep my distance from Washington, too. His people are all over Central Station. I intend to stay on my own."

"You're going to have to pick a side eventually," Polanski replied. "You can't hang out with this weirdo forever.

Washington's people can look out for you. Maybe make some kind of deal with Big Ben. Better than going over to Ivan, anyway."

"Always too smart for your own good, kid," she shot back. "You think Washington is such a prize? At least Ivan has the honesty to shoot you when you're looking right at him. With Washington, you never see it coming. He's always looking out for his own interests."

"Doesn't that make Washington the more honest one?"

Justine shook her head. "Fine, then. I couldn't even tell you why Washington repulses me. He just does. That doesn't make me Ivan's best friend. I want to stay independent. As much as I can, anyway."

Polanski shrugged. She could believe what she wanted to believe.

Justine looked at him. "So what are you going to do? Hang out with the Yids in the Middle Eastside? From what you were talking about last night, the odds don't look so good for you there."

Polanski put a hand right behind her ear and stroked the back of her neck. She looked away. "I can't stay here, that's for sure. Even if I could find all of my father's crew that survived, I'm not going to bring them back here. Better for them to hook up with Herzl or lie low in the Upper Westside. There's nothing left for us here, anyhow."

"So you're settled on your lost cause?"

"We'll make our stand in the only part of the City that's so godforsaken that none of the real bosses even want it. Maybe that's what will save us."

"Look, Gruber is gone now," Justine reminded, her voice breaking up just slightly, turning in towards him. "You really could stay. You could try."

"No, Justine," Polanski explained, pulling his hand back and turning away. "There's nothing left. I'm not coming back here for you. Not for some haunted memories. The Yids are ghosts in this place. And Central Station doesn't want us, no matter who's in charge here. That much is clear. So we're bugging out. We're going back to the one place that hasn't quite killed us all yet."

53

"You'll be back, kid," Justine whispered. A single tear came down her cheek. "You say you won't. But I know I'll see you again"

Polanski softened, just a tiny bit. "For now, all I've got to look forward to is a long time of fighting. What a war it's going to be. For a little patch of a street corner."

Boaz stepped into the courtyard through the mesh door. "Found you lovebirds. Alright, Polanski. Weissman's getting real prissy in there. We better go."

Polanski shrugged. He looked at Justine one last time. "That's it, then. So I'll see you."

She nodded without saying anything.

And that was it.

10
WAR ROOM

"Lucky" Lipschitz was having a very bad day.

Actually, he was dead. And his longtime moll, Avigail Berman, was only slightly better off.

The couple was dropped off on the corner outside the Citadel sometime early that morning.

It looked as though someone had gouged out both of Lucky's eyes with a hot spoon. The lower part of his right leg was only barely attached to the upper part. There was a string of ligament where his knee joint had once been. Both of his arms were broken and hanging off the body at weird angles.

And it looked like the bastards had done most of their wet work while Lucky was still breathing.

You could argue that Lucky got off easier.

Avigail's legs were caked in blood that ran from underneath her torn skirt. The hair on the back of her head was crispy and frazzled where her tormenters had set it on fire.

Now she stared at the world with glassy eyes, blinking only occasionally to show the spark of life was still somewhere in there.

Shank found them on the curb a half block down from the front door of the hotel. They might have been there for hours before the sun came up. The useless sentry at the front hadn't seen anything in the night.

There was no doubt who was responsible.

There was other news for the Yids that afternoon. Some was good. Most of it was awful.

Polanski, Boaz and Weissman had returned from their secret mission. That was good. They'd need every hand on deck for what was coming.

But the guns they'd purchased hadn't arrived yet. That was bad.

Word on the street was that the Muj were finally about to make their big push into Herzl's turf. That was very, very bad.

"Fariq's gang isn't waiting for Big Ben to pull out," Uncle Herzl told his crew, crowded into the big living room that now doubled as a war room. They peered over the crowded furnishings and clutter that filled up every nook and cranny of the ancient Citadel Hotel. It was an awkward place to hold a meeting, but such was the perennial problem for the Yids in the Middle Eastside. There was barely enough room to pretend like they had a normal existence, much less actually carry out the business of a working organization.

Some fearful faces peered into the packed area from the three directions. Herzl wasn't pulling any punches. Why would he? Better to tell everyone about the way it was.

"You've seen what they've done to us. They think the Middle Eastside belongs to them. Well, it doesn't. Big Ben is gone? Not here to hold the line between us and the Muj? That's a good thing. Us Yids are an independent entity. We declare it. And if anyone objects, then we fight for what's ours."

His gang nodded. They knew what Herzl had to say.

"We stand up for ourselves like any other gang in this City. We fight for our turf. And the Muj will take this place over our cold dead bodies."

The assembled felt their spines stiffen. Herzl was really getting into it now.

"Most of you already know the situation. We haven't heard anything from Karovsky's shop or Rorsach's crew. Lines are down. Fariq's already tightening the noose. They're going to attack tonight."

One old shlammer well past his prime was not convinced. "What are we supposed to defend ourselves with? Harsh language? And where are the guns the best of the best were supposed to bring in here? Far as I can see, we got bupkis." His outburst took the air out of the room.

"The merchandise is on the way," Weissman explained. "There were technical challenges with this shipment. Specifically, Big Ben's an ass."

The old man spat. "By the time it gets here, Fariq's boys are going to be the only ones standing around to sign for the shipment."

"Alright, that's enough, Popitz," Herzl commanded, his complexion turning dark. This was no time for debate. He had to rally the troops. "Sure, this situation is ferkakdeh. You think I don't see with my own eyes what's coming down on our heads? We're still gangsters. We're not little old ladies drinking tea, even if some of you lazy shnooks might invite the impression. Every last one of you is going to fight alongside me."

"Hear, hear!" the ones in the back shouted. "We'll fight with you, Uncle Herzl!"

Herzl continued trying to steel his unworthy crew. "We've done what we could to keep the peace when we could. And to fight back when we could. But we've never had the guns. Never had the numbers. We keep low. Try to make a buck. And those meshuga bastards won't let up."

"No more!" came the call from the back from an old and curmudgeony trigger-man of the last generation. The ancient wreck of a gangster was unfortunately par for the course in terms of the fighting prowess of Herzl's crew. But in the coming war, they would have to make use of anyone they could get.

"You're damn right, no more," Herzl answered. "Either we're the meanest sons of bitches in this neighborhood or they are. And if the guns don't come, we'll just have to be creative. Believe me, we've got a few tricks up our sleeve."

Zev Polanski stepped to Uncle Herzl's side. The boss graciously gave the kid the floor. "You Yids who've been here since before know what my crew went through in Central Station. You know we fought Gruber's shtarkes every inch.

"We lost. There's no getting around that. So we came here. We ran. We crawled. We came here and Herzl took us in. And we're damned grateful for that.

"But we've got nowhere else to run to. If Fariq's boys mop the floor with us when night comes, there's no running for the cellars and the sewers. You saw what happened to

57

Lipschitz and Berman. They will find the last of us and throw us into the harbor."

He wasn't Zev Polanski, "the kid", anymore. He wasn't some runaway with an outsized attitude. He was Uncle Herzl's enforcer. And he was going to set an example.

"Enough words," Herzl interrupted. "We've got a welcome to prepare for the guests we're expecting. The Muj better hope they don't manage to break in here. Because if they do, they will see how we fight when we're backed into a corner. Now who's with me?"

11

FIGHT CLUB

Night fell.

Big Ben's hard goons were long gone.

Now another force moved through the streets. Fariq's slavering thugs no longer clung to the shadows and the back alleys. They could operate out in the open. A long line of them filed through the main street of the Middle Eastside, surrounding the only building left for the Yids.

They carried torches. It was like in that old black and white Frankenstein movie with the villagers descending on the good doctor's castle. From afar, dancing flames played strange shadows of monsters and predators up on the stone walls.

On Herzl's orders, the storefronts and outposts further down the street had mostly been abandoned and shuttered before the sun went down. On a few rooftops and behind boarded-up windows beyond the Citadel Hotel, the Yids still held out. But there wasn't enough ammunition to go round to defend even Herzl's modest real estate holdings. So Herzl had gathered in his forces to where he knew they would be needed.

And as expected, Fariq's forces centered their attention on the Citadel Hotel.

Fariq had brought his whole contingent to the fight. They carried rusty pistols, shotguns and old farmer's rifles. Some would have to make do with axes or kitchen knives. Not quite an army. But certainly the biggest show of force the neighborhood had seen in some generations.

Nasser's men were conspicuously absent. Fariq had insisted on it, for the glory of his crew. His enforcers would be the ones to topple Herzl.

Nasser assented. He had always been more about real power than glory. Fariq was his puppet. So long as the Yids were beaten this night, his own men could mop up any of the last dregs. So he would let his attack dog have his bone.

59

Fariq gloated with a megaphone at those taking shelter in the Citadel. "Your protector is gone, Uncle Herzl. Big Ben has run from this place. But you should know that he did you one last favor before he left. I heard you were expecting a shipment from Central Station. It won't be getting here. There's no cavalry coming."

Listening inside the Citadel, Uncle Herzl grimaced. "Big Ben fucked us again," he whispered to Boaz, Zev and Chernik, close by him with guns already drawn. "It figures. So much for all of that protection money I paid out."

"We've got about six shots each before those bastards get in here," Chernik complained.

"Just make those shots count," Polanski answered. Once again, he showed the kind of force you'd expect from an enforcer at least ten years his senior; or at least from a guy who could grow a decent beard in less than a month. "The more of the Muj we get on the outside, the fewer we'll have to stab when they bust in."

"You got some big ideas, kid," Chernik replied nervously. "But let's get real, here. The Muj have got us surrounded."

"Look outside, Chernik," Herzl warned. "The kid might not be so crazy after all. There's not as many of the Muj as there should be. Looks like Fariq's trying to grab all the glory. I don't see Nasser's shtarkers down the street, do you?"

"That does even the odds a bit," Chernik said, taking heart. A little, anyway. "Maybe you're right, boss. Now we're only outnumbered three to one. How nice for us."

"Try to line 'em up in a row when you shoot to save bullets," Polanski said. No one was quite sure if he was kidding.

Boaz took his turn peering through the opening. "What do you want to do, boss?" Boaz asked, his squinty eyes focused on the besiegers outside. "Are we ready?"

Herzl shrugged. "Not much point putting this off any longer. Those cocktails ready topside?"

Boaz nodded. "The old cocksuckers and the molls are ready to throw down on your signal."

Fariq taunted them from outside.

"Come out, come out, wherever you are. Don't make this harder on yourselves, Yids. Tell you what, come out here and maybe we only kill half of you. The rest of you can work for me. Fair deal, no?"

Uncle Herzl had enough. "You're going to have to come in here and get us!" he shouted through the front door latch, pointing his gun out the tiny portal.

At the Yid boss' command, the electric lights went out through the whole building.

Fariq's lieutenant, Ansar, came close to his leader's side. "You sure about this plan, boss? The Yids have their place locked tight. We could wait for Nasser..."

Fariq growled and pushed the gangster aside. "Nasser had his chance. He could have come down here anytime since Herzl moved into this neighborhood. This is our night. And after tonight, there's going to be plenty of promotions to go around. You're looking at the new boss of this street."

"Then you give the word, Fariq," Ansar answered. "We're ready to go."

"Do it," Fariq shouted, pointing at the front door.

Ansar shrugged. "You heard the man," he called to the rest of the gang. "Go to it. Get those Yids."

Thus began the most incompetent gang assault ever conducted in the history of the City.

The torches Fariq's crew carried were a dramatic touch. But they also lit up his crew in the dark to make them easy targets.

The first crew with the battering ram didn't get ten feet before they were engulfed in a fireball from two Molotov cocktails lobbed simultaneously from the upper floors.

Twelve hoods got caught. They rolled on the ground in agony. The ones that didn't die in the next minute would not last out the morning.

Fariq's own gas bombs flung to the front of the stairs and the windows on the upper levels didn't get through. Most of the bombs chucked at the upper windows missed their mark, splattering flames on the stone walls to no effect. One bounced back, catching three of Fariq's gangsters in an orange explosion that was hot enough to melt metal.

61

Their lungs collapsed from the heat and melted before they had a chance to scream.

Gunfire from the Citadel dug into Fariq's numbers.

They were single shots from mostly ancient rifles and rusty pistols, with just a few decent weapons stolen from Big Ben's crew to round out the arsenal. And not every bullet found its mark. Misfires and jams rendered about a quarter of Herzl's arsenal useless.

But enough of the Muj gang crowded the street that those in Herzl's crew with functioning gats were bound to catch something. And they did. Just not enough to stop the enemy this early in the fray.

The Yids were in the unenviable position of needing to conserve their scarce ammo for a close-range to-the-death fight that could go either way.

Dodging over the still-smoldering bodies of their writhing comrades, a second and third street crew rushed in with a heavy steel pipe battering ram. Precision gunfire from the front of the Citadel hit them hard.

Whoever picked up the pipe at either end wound up with lead in their gut. This happened four times. Finally, the fifth team finally managed to join the swarm of shtarkes that had gotten up the front steps of the Citadel.

Ansar was one of the gangsters that had managed the feat. He'd saved a gas bomb to shut up the latch hole in the front door. From inside, Herzl's best trigger-men took turns blasting away at nearly point-blank range at the crowd of Muj shtarkes.

Ansar lit the wick on his bomb and shouted at the Muj thug in front of him to get out of the way. He needn't have bothered. Polanski's pistol dropped that hood before he had a chance.

Ansar now had the barest moment to do his business.

He hurled the bomb at the latch hole and it caught. It exploded instantly with most of the fiery explosion directed inside the front door.

Ansar and the shlammer beside him were caught in the blast as well. They fell in a blazing mess of barbecued flesh.

The gunman on the inside was gone, too, the remaining Muj could see. Killed or fled, it didn't matter. This was the opening needed for the battering ram to swing away.

Two burly shtarkes got on it. The door hinges buckled on the first blow. The second smashed the door inward, falling with a loud bang.

Fariq muscled in amongst his foot-soldiers that now stood on the verge of entering Herzl's lair.

A dark narrow hallway loomed before them, with rooms and a wide stairwell branching off to either side. The last bits of flaming debris from the gas bomb that littered the front entrance gave off haunting shadows along the walls. But the Yids had made themselves scarce.

"What the hell are you waiting for?" Fariq shrieked, lashing them onward. "Get in there and kill them all."

The next crew went down the hall, six men with guns drawn and wild eyes. A second team of enforcers started up the stairs. Fariq was frantic now. He screamed at them to get moving.

In the rush, it didn't take long for his shtarkes to set off the first traps.

A gas line in the kitchen rigged to go off with a tripwire incinerated seven of the invaders. Meanwhile, two buckets worth of chicken grease poured on the stairwell turned a dozen of Fariq's grim enforcers with murder on their minds into helpless sitting ducks.

Worse followed. Pipe bombs stuffed with broken glass and rusty nails. Chandeliers with spikes rigged to fall on the unwary. Little sticks of dynamite stuck into door handles, just enough to amputate a man's arm at the elbow. Snipers taking pot-shots from trap-doors in the walls with the defenders' last bullets.

Herzl had expected this assault for years. He'd refurbished the Citadel with these homicidal ideas in mind almost as soon as he'd taken ownership of the condemned building.

Some adjustments had been made in recent days to take advantage of the lethal ingenuity of the survivors from Central Station. But most of the carnage in that dark hour had to be credited to the dark and surreptitious mind of the owner of the building.

The traps would not completely thwart the advance of Fariq's sprawling legion of shlammers. But it would give the Yids a fighting chance.

Herzl's crew came back at Fariq's invaders with everything they had. Their last remaining bullets. Kitchen knives. Crowbars. Rusty axes. Even a cast-iron frying pan.

The fighting ran from room to room. The air was thick with blood-curdling screams and cursing all around. For some who had the misfortune to get too close, they could hear the sickening crunch of heads being smashed in with blunt objects.

Fariq's crew realized the cake-walk they'd been promised was a fiction. The hard core of them fought ferociously. But the Muj were fighting against a down-and-out gang that had been forced into a corner, with no way out.

The Yids had nothing left to lose.

And they fought to win.

Rivkah Livni pulled the lever on the generator in the basement one more time. The lights came on. The bodies of Fariq's hand-picked troop were piled in the halls.

Many of Herzl's crew would not last out the night. But the Yids had given far worse than they'd got.

Forty minutes into the brutal toe-to-toe fighting, it was apparent to anyone paying attention that the Yids were actually winning.

12
ONSLAUGHT

There was little time to lose. Herzl knew his forces had to press the advantage.

The attackers' weapons were taken up. Thirty-four guns, all told. Bullets were a bit scarce. Most of the intruders had at least managed to blast a few shots into the pitch dark before they were overcome. But it bolstered the Yids' meager arsenal significantly.

Fariq sprang to the window of a second-story horror chamber as Shank checked over what he thought was a corpse. The Muj street boss been stabbed in the gut. He had an inch-deep cut to his face that ran from his eye to his jaw. But he'd only blacked out. He wasn't dead. Not yet.

Fariq clipped Shank with an elbow and sent him to the floor, stunned and tasting blood in his mouth. Across the room, Chernik looked up from the shtarke he'd bludgeoned with a hammer. The mushy pulp of the victim's brains were still splattered on the edge of his weapon. He bounded after Fariq with a singular intent.

They were two stories up. But Fariq had lost his gun. And he was two seconds away from getting his brains smashed in.

He crashed through the window. He fell and landed on his left leg with a quease-inducing crunch.

Jagged bone ripped out of off his calf. A pair of his defeated hoods came to take him away. But he blacked out again.

Fariq had lost control. And there were no other enforcers with the juice or the initiative to lead the fight.

The survivors from Fariq's crew outside the Citadel Hotel were not top-ranked shlammers. These were the dregs, fit only for piling on to a four-on-one melee or gang-banging a skirt in a back alley.

The real Muj killers were inside the Citadel. And they were all dead.

Herzl quickly took command of a counter-attack on the beaten Muj shtarkes. On his command, the windows of the first two floors of the Citadel Hotel lit up with muzzle flashes from Fariq's commandeered weapons.

The volume of lead coming out of that first volley was enough to take down eight more of the shlammers at the perimeter.

At that, the retreat turned into a rout. Panicked Muj gangsters fled in all directions.

Polanski burst out of the front door, aiming and firing with a revolver. He took down two more of the enemy.

Boaz was right behind. He sprayed another cornered duo locked out of a storefront across the street with a shotgun he'd lifted off one of Ansar's shlammers.

The panicked thugs in Boaz' sights didn't even get a shot off before their guts exploded on the wall behind them.

Chernik emerged next with a rifle. He went hunting.

Blam! One went down. Then another.

Even Weissman got into the action. He juiced a gaggle of the Muj with a Mauser sub-machine gun. The weapon did its job before it jammed five seconds later.

"Give it to 'em, you lousy shtarkes!" Zev shouted to his comrades. "We've got them now." The Muj fled down the street, taking cover in back alleys and behind garbage dumpsters.

"Hold it," Uncle Herzl ordered. His fighters stared back at him, wondering if they'd heard right. "We got company." He pointed to the balding man from Central Station.

"Excuse me, friends," Tito interrupted as he lit up a cigarette. "But I've got a truck parked out back of the hotel with your merchandise."

"Bullets after the battle. Your timing's just great," Herzl snarled. "We've got people inside who won't see the morning."

"Big Ben got hold of one of my trucks," Tito excused himself with a shrug. "I apologize for the delay. You've got no idea what I've just been through."

"You've got some chutzpah. Herzl, do you want to shoot this putz in the head or will you allow me?" Polanski ripped.

"Look, do you want the merchandise or not?" Tito said, blowing smoke into the light of the neon sign. "Or I can bring it back to Central Station. Your choice. But I thought you Yids were reasonable people."

"All of you Yids, unload the truck," Herzl ordered. "We don't have time to argue with this mehuger. Fariq's down, but Nasser's still out there. And we've got no time to lose."

Chernik jumped up to the freight area in the back of the truck and started passing down semi-automatic rifles and boxes of ammunition to his fellow shlammers. Polanski sauntered over to Tito, cocking his shiny new Tommy gun. "Hey shnook! You don't mind if we borrow your truck to run a quick errand?"

Tito stared down the barrel of Polanski's weapon. "Please take it. Consider us even for the late delivery, yes?" He smoked his cigarette nervously, but did not look away from the cold-eyed kid with the rifle.

Polanski nodded. "It's a deal, putz. Alright, shtarkes. Pile in the truck. Let's take a ride and pay a visit to the Muj' boss of bosses."

Boaz insisted on getting into the driver's seat. Polanski shoved over to the cab passenger seat, pleased at the opportunity to literally ride shotgun. Everyone could see who was really in charge of this crew.

Herzl watched the kid take command as his older enforcers fall into line and chuckled. If only he'd had more street shlammers like this years ago.

They'd just have to make up for lost time.

13

ASSAULT

"You've brought shame upon us all, cousin," Nasser said. The defacto boss of the Middle Eastside looked down on Fariq with total contempt. His lieutenant was laid out there on a cheap folding chair in the basement. His roughly bandaged ankle bled on to the concrete floor.

Fariq's life was in no less danger for having escaped from the Citadel Hotel. Nasser was a dangerous man when he was angry.

Unfortunately for the Muj, it didn't take much to make him angry. And Fariq had done quite a bit this night, with very little to mitigate the extent of his failure.

Nasser was a big man, broad-shouldered and heavyset. He had the physique of an aging bodybuilder who'd only let himself go ever so slightly. His bulging arms and hard-done face still bore scars from his ferocious rise to the top.

Despite has position, he was always dressed only as well as his most poorly-paid shlammer. On this chaotic evening, that meant a starched white shirt and an ancient thin black tie, with creamy brown pants that frayed at the bottom. He wasn't precisely a man of the people; he just didn't see the point in wearing nice clothes that would inevitably get stained with blood.

Nasser was used to handling a lot of his own wet work in this very room. Problem was, Fariq was already too messed up. Between the ankle and a bullet wound, his cousin wouldn't be able to stand much punishment.

That didn't mean there were zero opportunities to demonstrate discipline. Nasser's fist rammed into Fariq's face. He knocked the bleeding man to the floor. A tooth bounced into the corner.

Nasser followed it up with a swift kick to Fariq's crotch. It came within a half pound of pressure of rupturing Fariq's sack. The poor shlub wouldn't be able to sit down for days.

Fariq begged for mercy. He pleaded on his knees, slobbering over Nasser's feet.

It didn't do him much good.

The boss kicked him back against the wall. One of Nasser's henchmen straightened Fariq up, just in case the boss felt like finishing him.

"You begged me to have the glory of kicking the Yids out of the Middle Eastside," Nasser hissed through clenched teeth. "And like a fool, I believed you could handle this little errand. Big Ben's gone, there's nothing to stop us from rolling in. But you managed to botch that somehow. The way I heard it, you went in and lit up the street like it was a holiday parade at night. Then you barge into their hornet's nest like a drunk fool."

"The Yids can fight," Fariq pleaded. "They're cunning. They fight like animals..."

Nasser struck him again. Fariq tried to shield himself from the blow with his hands.

Annoyed, Nasser kicked his lieutenant in the sopping bloody mess of the bandage near his ankle. Fariq yelped like a dog.

"You're weak," Nasser hissed. "I never should have protected you. The natural order's been upset. A stronger man would have risen in your place. Now I have to go in and clean up the mess you've left."

Fariq kept pleading for his life between moans of despair. But Nasser wasn't feeling particularly humanistic.

"You threw away half of your strength for nothing," he snarled. "Those Yid vampires at the Citadel Hotel are probably butchering them up right now. Grinding up the meat for their holiday pastries. So much for your glory. You're a loser, Fariq. The only thing keeping you alive is that all of the enforcers I'd replace you with are even more embarrassing."

Nasser motioned to his henchman standing ready. "Clean this loser up. We'll keep him around a little longer."

The goon nodded. He pulled up Fariq to shoulder height. The tortured Muj was too far gone to scream at his ankle gave out yet again.

Nasser put his hand on the henchman's shoulder. "Once you're done playing nursemaid for my cousin, you can join the rest of the crew. We're burning these Yids tonight."

The gangsters were distracted by the sound of a vehicle squealing its tires and revving its engine. Seconds later, explosions ripped the night.

Nasser looked up without comprehending. What the hell was going on? More booms, dulled by the thick concrete walls of the bunker. A machine gun dueled with semi-automatic gunfire around the same distance.

"What's happening out there?" Nasser snarled at his guards.

Fariq woke from his stupor, his eyes glassy and filled with dread. "It's the Yids. They're here…"

Nasser's eyes burnt with rage. "Get up there now. If Herzl's really stupid enough to send his crew here, it will save us the trouble of driving over to the Citadel."

His last thought was punctuated by another blast up top and the sudden smell of burning oil. The lights flickered in the stairwell.

Annoyed, Nasser bound up the stairs. The big picture flashed through his head and his blood pressure shot up.

If the Yids were really going on the attack, this was unprecedented. Ever since the Muj had exploded onto the scene in the Middle Eastside generations ago, the Yids had only ever fought rear-guard actions. For the most part, they just knuckled under. Only Big Ben and Francois' interference had let Herzl's crew get a toe-hold back in the Yids' old neighborhood.

If he didn't shut down the Yids now, that toe hold might become a permanent irritant; a spreading cancer. It could even undermine his own rule.

He'd made a critical mistake in letting Fariq move in without overwhelming force. He would have to end this now.

14

GUNS & AMMO

Nasser came up through the garage. The place housed his finely chromed fleet of armored cars shipped in from Central Station and the Upper Westside. The collection was the pride of his operation; not to mention a significant force multiplier for his enforcers.

As he opened the door to the motor pool, he was greeted by a ferocious wall of heat and smoke.

He slammed the door immediately. Not quite quickly enough. His eyebrows were singed. His face stung.

A mid-level thug bound towards them from the front entrance. "They Yids are tearing up the place! It's not safe here, boss!"

By this time, Nasser's face had darkened to a purplish hue with unmitigated rage. He pointed his pistol at the panicked thug's forehead at point blank range and pulled the trigger.

The Muj's brains splattered on the wall.

That caught the rest of the crew's attention.

There were five of them crammed into the hall, formerly running in a panic in all directions. Now they were too afraid to move.

"Who wants it next?" Nasser seethed, waving his weapon at all of them. "Get into the courtyard now and fight. Move!"

Nasser rallied his reluctant fighters into the lobby of his gang's fortress. The first goon to make it outside only made it five yards. He fell to his knees, a bullet lodged in between his ribs.

A second shot went through his neck, putting him on the ground before he could shoot back.

With the boss pointing a gun at their backs, there wasn't much of a choice. The rest of Nasser's foot-soldiers ran into the yard. They took cover behind shattered gun positions littered with the bodies of the first defenders.

The Muj fired back with whatever they had on hand; pistols, rifles, semi-automatics. Nasser strode forward, shooting into at the shadowy figures taking cover next to a freight truck. The targets were obscured in the distance by the smoke. But Nasser hadn't got to the top of his gang by missing his targets.

Bang! Bang! Bang!

He saw one of the figures drop. Nasser grinned from ear to ear.

A bullet whizzed past his forehead, nicking his right ear. Undeterred, he emptied the rest of his clip at the intruders before setting upon a still-functional machine gun. The operator was lying motionless to its side and missing half of his face.

Nasser pushed the carcass to the side and got to work.

"You come to my house and fuck with me here?!" Nasser swore, opening up with a long burst from the machine gun. "Fuck you, Herzl!"

Almost single-handedly, Nasser had turned the situation around.

Now his men streamed forward, blasting away at will. The accuracy of their firepower was cut down badly by the poor visibility from the smoking, wrecked vehicles in front and behind. But the Yids fell back under the withering storm of hot lead.

The last ones poured into the truck, screeching tires as hubcaps and windows shattered under a fusillade. The Muj kept pouring it on. With the aroma of burning rubber filling the air, the attackers were gone from the scene, melted into the street.

Nasser surveyed his holdings. The destruction was unbelievable.

Where the hell had the Yids managed to get their firepower? Who'd sold them the guns? That truck? Big Ben? Washington? Not Ivan, that was for sure. But then, that cold manipulative fucker had his own agenda... Nasser couldn't trust any of them.

Nasser turned to his ruined bunker. The motor pool was a total write-off. All those finely-tuned automobiles he'd acquired over the years were now hot blackened piles of scrap metal and melted rubber.

The west wing of the bunker was pockmarked with bullet holes and some of his men still slumped there. They wouldn't be getting up. He looked around and counted the bodies. Just in plain sight, nearly two dozen of his hoods, some of his best men, lay dead or dying.

It looked as though the assault had blown up two key gun positions en-route to the front door. But the other ones were untouched. Had his men simply run away?

Nasser's head swirled with fury.

They'd been beaten. And the Yids had got away.

Nasser stood up from the gun position and addressed the lieutenants who now drew close to him. He gave his orders through gritted teeth.

"You will bring me Assad. Get Bashir. Get every Muj street boss in the Middle Eastside. All of these bastards couldn't get their shit together for tonight. Tell them to get every last foot-soldier they've got and get down here now. And if they try to skip out, I will personally shoot each of them in the mouth."

His lieutenants scampered off. Nasser turned to the remaining foot soldiers.

"Uncle Herzl wants to draw us into a fight? We'll oblige him. Mark my words, men: we will throw these losers into the harbor before the night is out."

15

TOTAL WAR

The streets of the Middle Eastside now saw an epidemic of violence.

Nasser's men swarmed towards the Citadel Hotel from all sides. Herzl's prepared crews raked them with fire from the rooftops as they went. There would be no cakewalk for the Muj.

The Yids burned big piles of garbage in the streets to sting the invaders with smoke. The acrid stuff actually provided a bit of cover for the smarter ones among Nasser's crew. But it also made it virtually impossible for them to see Uncle Herzl's rooftop gunmen or the front-line shtarkes that scrambled from building to building in a deadly cat-and-mouse game.

Herzl's crews had made good use of the short hours after the raid on Nasser's bunker. They moved into the strategic buildings that Fariq's crew had mostly evacuated in the night. Fariq's mobsters thought they'd be able to just move back in with Nasser's forces backing them up. That tactical mistake opened up a world of hurt for the Muj invaders.

The road to David's Butcher Shop had gotten reinforced. The weight of Nasser's assault would mostly come from other directions. Still, Uncle Herzl was intent on taking the Muj stronghold. Taking out the gangsters held up there would give a tactical advantage. But for Herzl, it was more about giving the Yids something they could rally around. The Butcher Shop wasn't just another place they could run their rackets. It wasn't even just because that place was the seat of power of the most high-up Yid boss who had ever run things in the Middle Eastside.

For old-timers like Herzl that had come to the this borough back in the hard years, that was almost the only turf really worth having.

Polanski actually tried to talk Herzl out of it. "We're already trying to fight a war with just two truckloads of guns and a bunch of shlammers that can't shoot straight. Now you want to string us out along this road? Nasser's trigger-men are going to have a field day."

But Herzl was the boss. He was obsessed and the other old loyalists would back him up straight to the wall. "Even with that bald putz' weapons, were still outgunned. We're still outmanned. Kid, I've seen with my own eyes you got talent with a gun. But there's more to winning a war than marksmanship. Our shlammers need something to fight for."

"They already do, Herzl."

The boss shrugged. "You haven't lived here that long, kid. Maybe if we get through this, you'll see what I see. What we see. But we don't have time to run this war by committee. My orders are we go for the Butcher Shop. Do what you have to do."

Polanski grudgingly carried out his ludicrous orders. He brought over Bibi Waldman and his plucky street crew to secure the old brick two-storey blockhouse kitty corner to the Butcher Shop. And he directed the take-over of the parallel safe-houses where the Muj had skipped out, filling them up with guns and the thin-on-the-ground Yids who had enough skill to shoot.

Meanwhile, Nasser ordered his attacks.

Nasser shouted until his face turned purple. He cursed. He hissed. And through sheer force of will, he made the Muj shtarkes scramble into the darkened alleys, crash through barricaded doors and fight their way through the streets, house-to-house, room-to-room.

His foot-soldiers moved under an unseasonably dark and cold cloud overtop that blended with the acrid smoke of the fires. Where one Muj fighter was cut down by increasingly practiced sniper fire, three more would rush in. Block by block, his forces kept the pressure on Herzl's crews.

But the Yids weren't going down easy. And the dead kept piling up. Mostly, it was dead Muj shtarkes.

"You gutless muppet," Nasser cursed one bloodied foot-soldier who staggered out from an improvised Yid fort to the cover of a graffiti-splashed old stone wall. "Get back in there and finish them."

The foot-soldier fell to his knees, gasping for breath. He was barely aware of Nasser's pistol pointing between his eyes. "They got all of them... my brothers, the ones from the other street crew. They got 'em all."

"And I said, get back in there," Nasser insisted. He cocked his weapon for good measure.

The foot-soldier just stared back with glassy eyes. "They're shooting through the ceiling. Through the floor. You can't see them. And when you think you've got them cornered, they're gone."

"What do you mean, gone?" Nasser demanded.

"They've got tunnels. And ladders on the roofs. They know these streets. And they're just cutting us down."

As if to stress the point, Nasser watched as a burst of semi-automatic gunfire from a second-floor window perforated two of his cowering gunmen. They thought they were protected at the entrance to an alley. But from the angle the sniper was using, it turned out they had no cover at all.

Tunnels? Through the hard rock underground? Nasser couldn't believe it. But then, these Yids were cunning creatures.

How long had Herzl been preparing for this fight? Years? And now they'd finally gotten around Big Ben's blockades, these stubborn bastards had bullets to spare. Nasser's armored cars were melted slag. Had all those years of running away and acting like chickens been part of one colossal ruse? Was Herzl really that smart?

These thoughts flashed through Nasser's brain. His men had gotten soft from taking their grip over the Middle Eastside for granted. And in an even fight, the Yids were fighting smarter. They were using all the angles. They were hitting them.

The Yids could actually fight.

And maybe, if Nasser walked into their trap just like his useless stooge, Fariq, these bastards could win.

For the first time, Nasser felt a little chill in his spine. Things weren't going their way. He'd lost too many men.

Could they actually lose?

Nasser blasted away at the second-floor window with his pistol. The bullets only chipped away at the window frame. But the silhouette with the rifle barrel disappeared.

The fighting was getting seriously rough. And they weren't even approaching the Citadel Hotel yet.

Nasser saw another melee across the way. For a brief moment, he glimpsed a fat, burly Yid gangster hauling the limp body of the goon out to a fourth-floor fire escape. The Muj was still struggling. The fat man tossed the Muj over the railing like he was dumping garbage into the alley.

Astonished, Nasser watched as the Yid rubbed his hands like he'd just finished some woodworking and headed back into the apartment.

This fight was going all the wrong way. Clearly, a frontal assault was not in the cards. The Yids just weren't rolling over.

"Get back to the bunker," he commanded the pleading foot-soldier. "Pull back!"

He snarled at his startled crew. "Tell everyone to get back. The Yids want this street? They can keep it for a few hours. Get back, I said!"

Nasser glared at the smoke-filled street as his men pulled back and ran from shadows in doorways back to the end of the street.

His crew was in full flight now. To his chagrin, the Yids managed to pick off a few more of the retreating goons before they made it out of range. Their boss cursed and turned tail with his gang.

Nasser had thrown his full weight at the Yids and bounced back. So much for throwing their enemies into the harbor by the end of the night.

This fight was going to take a while longer.

16

SMOKE

Smoke hung in a gray haze across the City skyline to the southeast. For two days, the smoke swept in from unlucky wind into the low boroughs of the Upper Westside. Washington literally towered above it all, watching the scene play out from his office in the clouds.

At street level, the smoke got in your eyes and ears. And if you listened for it, maybe you could hear the rumble of an explosion or the stataco of automatic gunfire. Even from far away in the next borough, the war seemed close.

Many had expected the fighting to be over by now. But the Yids were putting up a good fight. They weren't rolling over.

Street crew bosses had noticed something else. Some of the Yids in their crews weren't showing up for work. They were usually pretty reliable. Now they were AWOL.

The theory was that they'd gone into the Middle Eastside to link up with Uncle Herzl's crew. Even some of the wimpy bagmen who had more in common with the fish than the shtarkes had taken off. And they'd taken their guns with them.

It wasn't just from the Upper Westside. Word was, the Yids were coming out of all of the neighborhoods. Not huge numbers. Nasser would still have them outnumbered, just about eight to one. The fight could still go sideways at any time. it might all be over any day now. But still, they went. Herzl hadn't even put out a call. But they were answering, anyway.

The bosses in Central Station were still trying to keep a lid on the action. After all, long-term disruption of the shipment routes was bad for business everywhere. But these interdiction efforts were only prolonging the fighting.

Reports from the lookouts near the action noticed Big Ben's crew were still trying to keep Ivan's guns out of the neighborhood. Some shipments were still getting through. All going to Nasser, no doubt. And Herzl wouldn't have the dough to match them.

Now Washington wondered if he'd made a mistake in turning away that kid and his entourage. If the Yids could pull it together, they could be useful.

More and more, it looked like Nasser was falling into Ivan's camp. Maybe he'd try something crazy. Cut off the flow of heroin, maybe? Or just jack up the price? If Nasser finally had a lock on all that turf, that could seriously hurt Washington's margins.

Maybe having Herzl as a counterweight to Nasser was something he ought to be thinking about. He considered it. But it was still too early. The war was too fluid.

The future was as hazy as the skyline.

Washington was not used to adapting to a fate assigned by others. He might yet have to intervene.

He needed more data. Who was actually winning in the Middle Eastside? Who was going to win in the end? And what was Ivan up to?

It was time to pay a call to his competitors.

17

STREET FIGHT

Six men moved in the darkness towards the shop on the west side of the street. Meanwhile, gun battles were raging on adjacent streets. At any moment, the battle might erupt around them. But they had come to bring the fight to the enemy.

All of the windows on the street were blacked out. It was too dark to see anything but the bulky outlines of buildings. If anyone was targeting these crouching figures as they huddled past, they would not know it until the gunshots sounded.

The six Yids made it to the other side without incident. They crouched beneath a window where a Muj sentry peered out the window, just missing them as they sought cover below.

Polanski lit the Molotov cocktail with a steel zippo lighter. He took a step out towards the sidewalk to get a decent angle; it wouldn't do for the thing to bounce and engulf them all in flame. He threw it.

Flames shot out from the second storey.

There was shouting from above. Screaming.

That was a good sign.

Boaz and Lipmann took their long section of iron pipe and rammed the front door. The frame buckled on the first hit.

Some Muj goon cursed at them from inside. He unloaded a shotgun blast prematurely, hitting only the inside of the door. The battering ram came again and the door came off its hinges, smashing straight into the guard.

Polanski strode in like he owned the join and finished him off with three rounds from his semi-automatic rifle.

Another one came down the stairs. It was one of Fariq's useless foot-soldiers, not from Nasser's better-trained crews. The guard tripped over his own feet, splashing face first in front of Chernik, who had grabbed the shotgun.

Boom!

The guard's head exploded.

The assault team raced into the building. Another guard got halfway down the stairs before Polanski blasted a burst into his gut. This one went down like the others. It was almost too easy.

That might have explained Chernik's risk-taking. He bounded up the stairwell three steps at a time, blasting his pistol into the first room. Flames from the Molotov cocktail still danced on the stone floor.

His own shots had no luck. But bullets from the other direction slammed into his chest. Chernik gasped and hit the floor.

Polanski cursed and went up the stairs after Chernik. He stayed low. Two shots ricocheted off the wall near where the top of his head had popped up. Then he heard a distinct click, like from an empty clip.

He came up a bit more, spraying the room. A thug holding himself up against a crate grunted with pain. Polanski had hit the bastard in the wrist and the chest.

Polanski reloaded his own weapon as Boaz came up past him into the room.

One of Fariq's boys was still ready to go. He shot at Boaz at nearly point blank range. But the first shot only grazed Boaz' shoulder. His gun jammed on the second shot. That was pretty much it.

Boaz cracked the man's jaw with the butt of his rifle. He wasn't going to waste bullets on this shnook. He clubbed him again. Now the blood was flowing. One more time with the rifle butt.

The last fighter's brains were splattered all over the floor.

Boaz noticed the one that Polanski had only wounded. He gave him the same treatment.

Lipmann, a hard-boiled shlammer with a chiseled jaw just arrived from the Upper Westside, checked Chernik over. "Looks like the bastards got him."

"Chernik deserved a better end," Boaz cursed. "Poor Rivkah. She's going to be heartbroken."

81

"We won't have much time," Polanski reminded them. "What's in those crates?"

Lipmann found a crowbar and pried one open. "The boss was right. Man, you're not gonna believe this."

There were boxes of ammunition for heavy weapons three rows deep. They opened up another crate. More ammunition, plus heavy rockets and a big box of grenades. The crew's eyes widened with each new discovery.

"Where's Nasser getting all this?" Samberg asked. He was a skinny shlammer, more like a new fish than a gangster. He was one of Uncle Herzl's loyalists from way back in the day. Now he was working on the front lines.

It couldn't be helped. The turf war was very quickly draining off the already thin cream of the Yid's forces. More and more, front-line enforcers had to rely on the kind of squishy hired help that specialized in manufacturing and fencing knock-off goods, not mixing it up on the streets. But he had a pulse and a trigger finger. It would have to be enough for the rest of this war.

"Looks like Big Ben's manufacture," Polanski replied with a frown. "Look, there's his stamp. But this here could be some of Gruber's old stock. And some of it's from the Upper Eastside. No way to know how much of it is new. But it's not a good sign. Herzl's going to be pissed."

"This stinks," Lipmann said with a scowl. "Our side's got no decent supply. And Nasser's still got a lock on all the shipments into the Middle Eastside. How long are we supposed to fight like this?"

Polanski grimaced. "Let's leave the big picture up to Herzl. We've only got a few minutes before they figure out what happened and the cavalry shows up to kick us out of here. We can't take this with us."

"You want to just leave all this behind?" Samberg asked, screwing up his face into a weird grimace. "There's enough for an army here. We can't even get to Bibi's place now and they'll have a clear line to them. They won't last much longer. And we'll be next."

"Nah, the kid's right," Boaz admitted. "We don't have time to set up a proper position here. The Muj could get a drop on us at any time. We'll take what we can and get back. "

"We'll leave a surprise, though," Polanski added. "Let's make those putzes work for every inch they take from us."

The crew got to work. Half guarded the entrances to the building. The others set the trap.

They couldn't try anything fancy. It wasn't like Herzl's gang was overflowing with bomb engineers. But they had enough material to work with. They could afford to be crude.

A new sound startled them. It was the rotor of helicopter blades flying above the street. "What the hell?" Samberg asked.

"Can't be Nasser," Polanski reasoned. "Ivan's, maybe. Or Washington's. You can't get that kind of hardware here. No way."

"What the hell are they poking their noses here?" Lipmann rejoined.

"We caught someone's attention," Polanski answered. "Could be a good thing."

"Fucking weird is what it is," Boaz stated, coming back into the room. "I think it's leaving. Alright, we're set. Let's go."

Boaz carried Chernik's bullet-riddled body. The rest of them humped ammo.

The team made it out the front door just as another of Fariq's rough crews came in the back.

The Yid crew was nearly on the other side of the street when Samberg dropped a box of bullets. It landed on his toes.

He let out a yelp. That was an awful thing to do while trying to extract themselves with a bit of stealth. And it got noticed.

The first of Fariq's shlammers to get into the second-storey office aimed his rifle into the inky blackness. He pointed his weapon at the direction of the sound. There, he saw just a little movement.

Crack!

Polanski dropped, clutching his head. Pain exploded out of the left side of his face.

Boaz saw the kid go down and cursed. "When are those damn charges going off?"

More shots from the building bounced off the pavement. The Yids fired back at the windows.

Polanski was staggering, about to black out. Boaz hauled him up on his other shoulder next to Chernik. He got them behind a low curbside wall.

Finally, their preparations did what they were supposed to do. Better late than never.

Every window on the second storey of the building blew outward with a fireball. Fariq's men were incinerated instantly. The building lit up the night sky.

The helicopter that was hovering nearby was rocked by the force of the blast. It maneuvered up, escaping back in the direction of the Upper Westside.

Meanwhile, the flames spread to the adjacent buildings on the west side of the street. That's where a motley combination of Nasser and Fariq's boys had also set up shop. Panicked, some of those foot-soldiers ran out into the night.

Lipmann and Samberg unloaded on them from across the street. They managed to drop three of them.

Polanski was awake again, groaning. Boaz looked at the kid in the flickering light. The left side of his face was sticky red from an awful wound to his eye.

"I can't see shit, boys," the wounded fighter complained, his voice still retaining most of its hardness.

"You're going to be alright, kid," Boaz said.

"Fuck, this hurts bad."

"We'll get you back to the Citadel. Don't worry about a thing."

"Fuck those Muj shtarkes. I hope they all burned in there."

"We got 'em, Polanski. No doubt about that."

The rest of them looked at the burning building they'd left behind. The flames lit up the entire street. For a moment at least, the battle was halted. Both sides took in the spectacle with an equal measure of awe.

Meanwhile, the helicopter heading off in the distance.

They'd made some kind of an impression. Maybe, just maybe, it would be enough to get them some breathing room.

18

JAW JAW

The shiny chrome Rolls Royce pulled up to the front of the United Hotel. It had stylish steel plating and tinted bulletproof windows. And the surroundings were at least as defined by sophistication and security.

The squat tower loomed over the waterfront in the Upper Westside. The place took up two city blocks. Its gray concrete edifice was particularly awe-inspiring. Flags representing all of the City's boroughs stood in the driveway.

The occupants stepped out of the car. The wind and rain had picked up a notch. Over the pitter-patter, you could only barely make out the thunder of battle back in the Middle Eastside. Uncle Herzl pulled up the collar of his old coat to keep the weather out. He resented that the huge shtarkes on either side of him made him look like a dwarf. He could use some big guns like that in his crew.

Inside, the hotel was even more impressive. Bright lights and polished brass invited them into the ornate lobby. A giant map of the whole City detailed down to the tiniest intersection covered the wall to the left. To the right, the foyer opened up into a gold-gilded bar complete with knockout cocktail waitresses and cigar-smoking bigwigs. They were mostly from the ritzier parts of town. But Herzl recognized a few distinguished trigger-men from the Upper Eastside.

Washington was there to greet him, complete with an entourage of a dozen of his biggest gorillas. Puffing on a cigar, the master of the Upper Westside extended him a hand. "Glad you could make it, Herzl. The party's about to start."

Herzl was still a bit awestruck by his lush surroundings. His status as a boss in the Middle Eastside had been accrued over decades of bootstrapping, long-term planning and self-promotion. But he'd never felt like he really belonged among the bosses from the other boroughs.

"I've never been here before, you know," he admitted. "These are some fancy digs."

"I don't really own the United Hotel," Washington noted with a shrug. "Consider it a public amenity. I just keep the lights and plumbing working and set up the meetings."

"Everyone's here already?" Herzl asked.

Washington nodded. "They're waiting for you," Washington answered. "They're very eager to get to know you, Herzl. You might say this is long overdue."

"You might say," Herzl repeated.

The boss of the Yids took his seat at the long table. The hard liquor flowed and soon they got into it. Cigar smoke and testosterone permeated the room.

A swarthy, pot-bellied bald Muj sat across from him. He seemed unusually refined for one of Nasser's employees. Meanwhile, other representatives from the other boroughs had come in for the occasion. But they were mostly just for show.

There were plenty of interested parties. But there were only going to be two sides to these negotiations to end the war.

"Nasser was too busy to make it?" Herzl asked. "Who the hell are you?"

"I work for Mr. Nasser," the fat man across from him answered. He spoke with a lisp that Herzl found immediately annoying. "My name is Rahim. These are delicate matters between our two organizations, Mr. Herzl. It was deemed inappropriate for my boss to take part in these negotiations directly."

"No kidding," Herzl answered, already pissed off at the thought of talking with Nasser's underling. But he couldn't say no to this meeting. "I take it you're authorized to make this deal?"

"Mr. Nasser has provided me with full instructions," the fat man answered. "May we begin?"

"Let's get to it, Muj," Herzl replied. "What are you offering?"

"Mr. Nasser is prepared to offer you a comprehensive ceasefire along the line of current holdings of our organizations," Rahim stated without a hint of emotion. "This agreement is to go into effect at midnight tonight."

"What else?" Herzl asked, suspicious of the easy terms.

"Over the next forty-eight hours, your people will vacate all buildings formerly under Fariq's management," Rahim continued.

"I figured that," Herzl answered. "Out of the question. Your 'organization' started this meshugaas to put us out of business permanently. What about my store-fronts where you've set up shop? I'm supposed to just let you keep them? That's some chutzpah you've got."

"Mr. Nasser's position is that these very limited holdings are a down-payment on compensation owed by your organization for disruptive business practices," Rahim shot back without so much as a smirk.

"This gets better," Herzl replied. "What sort of total compensation is your boss looking for?"

"Mr. Nasser will be satisfied with a transfer of the deed for the Citadel Hotel and all of your adjoining properties along your street. Your continued residency in our territory will be conditional on a lease-hold agreement by which your business assets will become title of our organization."

"Right," Herzl answered. "You couldn't beat us outright. So now you want to swindle our street out from under us. No deal. Fuck your boss. You can tell him that."

A pang of unpleasantness came into his gut. He couldn't agree to the terms. But the situation on the ground was looking worse by the hour. Ammunition was running low. Most of his shlammers hadn't slept in three days. His best trigger men were about done. Polanski was half-blinded and probably on his way out. Chernik was dead. The bodies of his foot soldiers were stacking up.

And Nasser still had a lock on the smack trade, giving him a leg up on every other boss in the City. Time was working for the other side.

"I would urge you to accept these generous terms," Rahim insisted. "Let it not be said that our side was the impediment to the proper functioning of business in the Middle Eastside."

That was too much. "I will say it," Herzl replied, getting more irritated at the minion's awful lisp. "I'm saying it now. No deal. No fucking way. It's ferkakdeh."

At this, the representatives from the other boroughs blanched. Argument erupted between Big Ben's faction and Ivan's lobby. Washington tried to get them to tone it down, to no avail. In the meantime, Herzl and Rahim kept needling each other.

"This isn't just about you gentlemen," Washington stammered. The assembled gangsters paid heed. "Let's face the facts. The trade routes and commodities in the Middle Eastside are vital for all of us. This war is diverting too much effort from the management of shipments. We all want these battles over with as soon as possible.

"On the other hand, as my colleague from the Upper Eastside will attest, we are not just in our respective enterprises for the profit motive. Each player in our game has earned a place at this table. And that includes our friend Herzl and his crew."

"That is a matter of opinion," Rahim interrupted.

Washington ignored him. "If we allow one of us to be cheated out of his proper holdings, the rest are at risk from similar litigation-style business practices. Competition in a free market is the only proper way of doing things. There will be winners. And there will be losers. If either side has gained market share in the Middle Eastside through our age-old rules of competition, we should abide by the results."

"What are you suggesting, then?" Ivan's representative queried. "Neither of our astute colleagues seems interested in a deal."

Washington shrugged. "In the short term, all that is required is that the Middle Eastside become quiet again. The simplest solution is a ceasefire along existing lines of control. The rest of the details can be sorted out later."

Rahim stroked his chin. "I am authorized to offer the terms of this ceasefire in stages," he suggested. "Of course, it would be incumbent on Mr. Herzl to ensure that the latter points of this agreement were implemented in due course... or his organization will be deemed responsible for the outbreak of any future hostilities."

"This seems eminently reasonable," Francois' bagman from Central Station summarized. "Good enough for us, then. Herzl? What do you say?"

Herzl looked around the table at the unfriendly, unsmiling faces; the scheming betrayers from Central Station; the hostile lobby from the Upper Eastside; Washington, pursuing his own agenda and balance of power with his adversaries at the table; and that fat, cold, effeminate flunky sitting across from him, who'd sooner slit his throat than keep talking with him.

So the decision was already made for him.

It wouldn't be peace. But it wouldn't be war, either.

Perhaps it could even last a little while.

19
A KIND OF PEACE

Zev Polanski had an awful pain in the swollen left side of his face. Chernik's young widow, Rivkah Dudek, was changing his bandage. She cleaned up the blood and goop from the horror show where his left eye had once been. It was a torturous process for both.

While she wrapped the white cloth around his head, Polanski touched her arm.

"Chernik gave those shtarkes hell before he went," Polanski said. "He was a good Yid."

Rivkah continued bandaging him up. She didn't answer him. She didn't seem particularly moved by his eulogy, either. Her grief still too fresh and she was keeping it locked inside for fear of breaking down entirely.

Polanski let her finish up without bothering her again. In a little while, she left him in the dark. She'd come back to look in on him in a bit. But there were many other broken Yids to patch up this night.

He must have gotten at least a few hours sleep. It wasn't real sleep, what with the pain and the noise and the stress they all breathed in the dark rooms of the Citadel Hotel. He'd blacked out from pure exhaustion.

But there was something different when he woke up. He couldn't quite put his finger on it. It was still dark. It still stank of sweat and rotten guts. And when Rivkah came back, she was still had the same sad, tired eyes he'd seen hours before; a look that contrasted much with her usual happy expression. Then again, these last few days had been tough on the looks of even this stoic set of Yids.

Then he realized what it was.

"It's too quiet," Polanski muttered. "What the hell happened to all that racket? Where's the fighting?"

Rivkah looked at him with a frown. "You slept through it. The boss came through. The war's over."

Polanski couldn't quite believe it. How had it happened? And what was going to happen now?

For the first time in many months, a shadow lifted from Polanski's brain. The threat of imminent extermination no longer hung over him. What was this strange thing that loomed before him? A life? A life for what?

His brain clicked over from something geared for tactical survival to something that could let go, at least for this moment. It was a strange thing to once again be able to think of tomorrow.

The pain bothered him. His hand moved to where his eye had been.

Rivkah moved it away. "Don't touch it. It looks horrible. I'm going to cover it up so you don't scratch it in your sleep."

"You've got a real bedside manner, Rivkah."

"Just stay still for a second. I'm going to put a patch on you."

"Herzl could have done this deal before those shtarkes took out my eye. What's it look like?"

She shrugged. "What do you think? Look, you're not the only one who's lost something."

Polanski felt even worse than before. "I'm sorry about Chernik. I shouldn't have said that."

"It's alright. You're entitled." She wrapped the gauze and covered up his wound again. Once it was in place, she let just a bit of a smile show. Maybe she was proud of her work.

"You know what this means?" he said, pointing at his eye.

She shook her head without talking.

"I'll be a pirate. The first pirate gangster in the Middle Eastside."

She smiled more fully at that. But it was still too soon. The sadness returned to her face in an instant. Rivkah and Chernik had only been married for two months. And now it was over before they'd even had a chance to really have a life together. The future in her mind was now a blurry shadow.

92

Polanski pleaded with her to stay with him. He was no longer the cool trigger-happy gangster prodigy of Central Station. Now he was just some young shlub with a messed-up face. And he knew it. For the first time in a very long time, his vulnerability was showing through.

She stayed with him a little while longer. She pressed her hand into his. For a moment at least, the pain in Polanski's head was swept away.

Then she left to help bandage up some other poor shmuck who had the bad luck to get clipped before the clock ran out on their war.

There'd be many more before the day was through.

Polanski closed his eyes and tried to distract himself with thoughts of Rivkah while the opium wore off. The awful searing pain in the ulcerous socket of his left eye slowly drifted back. It pressed all thoughts of his nurse away. Instead, his head was filled with bad memories.

In his pain, he thought of the darkness and the horror of the underground in Central Station. The repressed claustrophobia of the cellars and the stink and the misery of the sewers came back.

He thought of his father and the good men who'd saved him. And the ones he'd helped save. He thought of how most of them ended up even after all that effort.

Dead in the gutter. No one to remember them, except perhaps their killers.

He pushed those thoughts away and tried to settle on something that might relieve his pain.

Again. Rivkah's sweet face flashed into his mind, but only briefly. It wouldn't be enough.

So his thoughts drifted again.

Now he imagined the old Butcher Shop as it might have been those countless years ago.

His fellow Yids gambled at the tables. They drank whiskey and cognac served by soft-skinned cocktail waitresses. Shlammers from all over the City hung around at the front deli of the shop. They smoked cigars and held court over thick rolls of pastrami and roast beef.

In this place, strange and familiar at the same time, there was an impression of security. It was like the feeling he'd experienced a moment ago, when Rivkah held his hand. Here in the Butcher Shop, the Yids could not just rule the roost; not just do business in the day light; they could live like real people. They could just be like any other gang in the City, in a way that they'd never been able to be when they were holed up at the Citadel Hotel.

As quickly as it had arrived, the vision went away.

The morphine was done. And the pain was like a burning fire in his skull.

He spent the rest of the night awake, feeling the pain. He had the feeling that he would never quite get used to it. He'd always have that pain with him as a reminder of what he'd been through in the first war with the Muj of the Middle Eastside.

But maybe that was a good thing.

PART 2
1956

20
LIVING UNDERGROUND

Nasser was in a dark mood. He had been in one for years. His office in the deepest, darkest section of his bunker stank of stale cigar smoke, sweat and failure.

There were no books or television sets or other distractions in this place. There was just Nasser; a thwarted boss drinking in the sting of defeat. He swam in the dishonour of banishment to what he perceived as second-class status in the Middle Eastside.

The Muj weren't used to playing off their back foot, Nasser told himself for the ten thousandth time. Or was he living in the past? The Muj had exploded over the Middle Eastside generations back. They'd even made inroads into Central Station and the Upper Eastside. And now they were getting their asses handed to them by a gang that was supposed to have been put out of business permanently back in that initial conquest.

Every Muj knew the stories of how their gang had taken control. The other gangs were on the decline after a turf war like the City had never seen. The Muj won their position by operating according to simple rules. The City was basically split into a place for the Muj and a place of war. Outside gangs could never be allowed a toe-hold on Muj turf. The basic strategy was to attack the outsider whenever opportunity allowed; honour ceasefires only for as long as it took to rearm; and in areas where the Muj were in charge, any fish that remained either swore a blood oath to the Muj boss of the time or got their throats slit. To be fair, all of the other gangs operated according to similar principles. But the Muj took these rules to the extreme.

But the Muj were on the defensive, now. Their total intransigence, maximalist claims on turf and never-ending list of ceasefire violations was fine for gaining ground when they held an advantage. But it was awful for forging alliances necessary to hold onto their gains.

That was pretty much how the bosses of Central Station had managed to set themselves up in the Middle Eastside in the first place. Bosses like Big Ben and Francois were still influencing events in the borough after generations of living only on the outside. And now Herzl's plucky crew of Yids was firmly entrenched.

It was an absolute embarrassment.

As Nasser considered these thoughts for the umpteenth time, he was interrupted by a knock on his door. The guard let his visitor stand at the entrance.

"What the hell do you want?"

"It's Fariq," said his crouching lieutenant, his silhouette stuck in the doorway. He was still the very much alive street crew leader of the slum on the northeast sector bordering the Yids; unfortunately. "I have an idea."

"As good as your last one?" Nasser growled. The stink of defeat had just gone on to a whole other level as Fariq came in. "How many ways will your schemes end in me getting fucked in the ass?"

Fariq shrugged. "I can come back later."

"No, stay," Nasser insisted. He picked up the revolver on his desk and started loading it with bullets one at a time. "Amuse me, cousin."

"I have a plan for war by other means, boss."

Nasser sat up. What the hell was his cousin on about? "You want us to go hit up the Yids again? How unexpected. How very innovative. You're such a tool."

"You hear what I hear," Fariq said. "Our enforcers are restless. They want a fight. And they don't understand why we're holding them back. And these days, I don't understand it much either."

"Your impatience worked real well for us last time," Nasser reminded with a scowl. "How's your leg these days?"

Fariq ignored the jibe. "This wouldn't be another turf war. But we have to do something. The Muj didn't take this neighborhood in the first place by sitting on the sidelines."

Nasser shook his head. "We also didn't win by running into battle before we were ready. You want to send the rest of your crew out on a suicide mission?"

"I've got a crew ready to go," Fariq insisted.

Nasser had finished loading his gun. He pointed it into the darkness wide of Fariq and pretended to pull the trigger. "What have you got planned?"

"It may be suicide like you say. But these boys won't mind dying. I didn't recruit them. They came to me. Just so long as they get to fight the Yids. It's about honour. Something you used to know about."

A deadly silence ensued.

It lasted for a full minute.

Finally, Nasser began to laugh.

At first, it was brooding, like a whisper.

Soon, it reverberated off the walls, echoing down the halls. The eerie sound haunted the gangsters who stood around in the bunker.

"You're a funny man, Fariq," Nasser started. "A joke. You don't know fuck about waging war. About discipline. About what it takes to build an empire.

"All these years later, after all the advantages I gave you, you're still thinking like a common thug. You think you're a real gangster because you've done a little killing. I know about killing. I got to where I am from swimming in a river of blood."

His tone was full of condescension now. "You think I'm waiting around for the hell of it? We have to learn from the outsiders. They stored up their strength before they made their treacherous moves against us and put us in this position. We're building up so the next war will be what the last war was supposed to be. I have no interest in fighting the Yids. My interest is killing them.

"That's why you see our deals we're working on with Ivan. Taking control of the waterfront. We're going to have full control, lock out the stooges in Central Station and the Upper Westside. Lock in the Yids here with us until we're ready to put them in the ground at once. This is what real warriors do. This is how you run a gang."

Fariq would not give up. "We see the strategy. But we don't see an end to it. We're gangsters. We didn't sign up to sit around in cafes and knock over our own fish. I ask you, Nasser, when are you going to go on the attack? Are we gangsters or not?"

Nasser gritted his teeth. "You really think you can do this without setting off Herzl?"

Fariq shrugged. "Would you really be so mad if we did? You're already talking about locking down the harbor. If my volunteers don't set off those bastards, what do you think your grand strategy is going to do, boss? Besides, if the Yids declare war, we'll get the rest of the City behind us."

Nasser considered that. It was possible. He could turn the tables on the Yids. They were only able to survive in their corner of the Middle Eastside with the sympathy of outsiders. He could break that link.

His gang might not be ready for an all-out fight. But if it happened, some back-room diplomacy could make up for a gang that couldn't shoot straight.

"Maybe you've got some strategy in you after all, cousin," he thought out loud.

"I'll tell the crew."

Nasser nodded. "We'll test the waters. Maybe it is time to flex our muscles. Let's see what they've got."

21

BROKEN PROMISES

Most of the offices and shop fronts across from Zev and Rivkah Polanski's apartment were on Fariq's turf. It made for a bad view.

Scores of Nasser's foot soldiers died taking those buildings. But the Muj boss had given them over to the crippled Fariq to manage on his behalf. And there was no cash to patch them up after hostilities ended. Every last dollar from the heroin trade got funneled right back into drugs for customers in Central Station and the Upper Westside. That, or the flood of guns coming in from Ivan's turf.

Year after year, the patches of street where Fariq's crew were holed up transformed into a filthy broken-down slum. A good number of them slept on the street. The bums had only newspapers and rubbish for cover.

Sometimes violence would erupt from within those holdings. There were random stabbings and gunshots. Sometimes, an explosion would rock the Middle Eastside. Fariq's boys would fight among themselves. They did just about everything they could to reinforce Nasser's perception of this unruly mob as worse-than-useless cannon fodder.

And then there were the other kinds of internal incidents. Nasser's street crews beating one of Fariq's poor useless beatniks for some minor transgression. There was no recourse for these kinds of happenings.

Sometimes Fariq's boys let off steam outwards. There would be a pot-shot against the Yids in direct violation of the ceasefire agreement. Fariq would go through the motions of disciplining his wayward foot soldiers with a bullet to the knee or a hammer coming down on an outstretched hand. These incidents were just isolated enough that both sides could avert a full-scale turf war.

But the last few weeks, they Yids had seen something different. Shlammers from Fariq's holdings were hitting out almost at random. Some of these rogue Muj trigger-men got smoked by Polanski's increasingly vigilant street crews before they got close. But some would make it in and manage to rough up a joint. A few would even leave one of Herzl's boys dying in the gutter.

But with these cases, Nasser kept his distance, insisting these were gangsters didn't belong to his operation. You couldn't pin down the bastard with anything. And word was coming out of Fariq's slums that there was a new gang operating there. They were the Fedayen. They'd split off from the main gang. Now they were trying to make a name for themselves at Herzl's expense.

The violence was getting worse. But actually, it was still an improvement from what the Middle Eastside had been like before the war. The main difference was that the Yids had guns.

Just as worrying for the Yids were Nasser's increasing threats to block off the harbor. It was already tough enough for the Yids to move product in and out of the Middle Eastside. And if Nasser followed through with his provocations, he was going to make it tough for the rest of the City.

Meanwhile, the rest of the neighborhood had improved under Uncle Herzl's stewardship. The Yids had increased their real estate holdings. It wasn't much of a gain, but it was enough to give them contiguous sections of neighborhood blocks. Consolidation provided just enough security to help the internal underworld market to really get things going.

Herzl had far less turf than Nasser. But he had a more effective management style that didn't involve summary execution of poorly performing goons who pissed him off. He trained his gangsters up. In some ways, he was more like a fish entrepreneur than a hood. The Yids were almost prospering.

Herzl's business had really taken off when he got into the development business to facilitate lucrative protection rackets in a dense neighborhood. He put up five-storey towers to house the Yids who were still coming in from the outer boroughs. There were even new trees planted in rows along the shop fronts. It was even kind of pretty. And the rest of Herzl's neighborhood was kept up by his industrious fish.

In the heart of those developments, Rivkah Polanski petted the leaves of the little fern on the balcony of their tiny apartment.

Their place overlooked the street with the Butcher Shop at the very far end and to the left. That view directly in front had declined over the years. The slum stretched on for as far as they could see. "The Muj must have a better view from where they are," Rivkah said.

Zev Polanski came up behind Rivkah. He looked completely different from when they'd first met in Herzl's kitchen. The rail-thin rogue with his belt notched up to its tightest rung was gone. Only his peircing look that could charm or intimidate at will remained.

Now he was a hard man with thick arms, a washboard stomach and permanent stubble. Years of bloody-minded physical training and twelve hour days as a hard-knocking street-level crew boss had transformed him into one of the toughest enforcers in the entire Middle Eastside.

The black eye-patch gave him a bit of panache that made the other gangsters jealous. The wound never really stopped bothering him. The pain from it never went away.

Naturally, he was hooked on morphine. Right at the moment, it coursed through his system. His senses were a bit dulled. He was almost mellow.

"They can have their view," Zev replied. "I prefer ours. We paid a high price for it. But it's worth it."

He slung his hand around her waist. She smiled back at him. He looked down and petted her growing belly.

She'd started showing about two months ago.

Rivkah pushed his hand away gently. Already, the kid was coming between them.

"You think they could threaten us again?" she asked, frowning.

Zev wasn't one for sugarcoating things. "We're going to have to fight them sometime. And we can win a hundred times. They only have to beat us once."

He pulled away. He was already thinking of something else.

"Where you going, baby?"

"Bike's been acting up lately," Zev answered, pulling on his steel-toed boots. "Throttle's twitchy. It's stalling in third gear. Ever since I put in those cheap shocks from the Eastside. Looks like I need to build all my own parts."

Rivkah frowned. "You know Boaz wants us to come by his place later. He says you've been dodging him. You'll have time for that, right?"

Zev shrugged. "Boaz spends all his time sucking up to Herzl. Ever since I got tapped to head up the main street crew, your pop's been hard to take."

"You're imagining things," Rivkah shot back. "Daddy doesn't have it in for you."

"Fine, I'm imagining things," Zev said. "You know he's never been happy that we ended up together. He thinks you're too good for me."

"I am," Rivkah replied with a mischievous smile. "Don't you know that yet? You hit the jackpot, Zev. I'm the only moll in this whole place who'll fuck a one-eyed thug."

"What a coincidence? That's why I married you."

"Fuck you."

"Hmmm," Zev said. "Maybe later. See you for dinner."

He hopped down the metal stairwell to the garage. His shocks needed some work.

22
OPPORTUNITY KNOCKS

Polanski listened to the growling hum of the motorcycle engine in neutral. Something was definitely off.

It wasn't the shocks. Or maybe the shocks were off and now something was knocked loose in the intake valve. He frowned. No way around it. He turned off the engine.

He'd just have to take it apart again and figure it out.

"It's those damn cheap parts we picked up from the Eastside," Shank complained. "We've got to get some of that good shit Washington's producing. It's pricey but at least it works. His fish work wonders."

"Fuck Washington," Polanski replied. "Nasser won't even let his good stuff into our neighborhood, anyway. We can make these parts and hock them on the market ourselves."

"We expecting company, boss?" Shank asked his eyes drawn to some silver limousines hugging the road towards the Citadel from the west side. The flags markers on the hood showed Central Station gang colors.

The hair on the back of Polanski's neck was on edge. Who would be coming to the Citadel now?

Polanski kept his grip ready on the revolver tucked into the back of his blue jeans.

He was joined in front of the hotel by a half-dozen other trigger-men with fedora hats and Tommy guns. Times had changed from when Herzl's crew had to ration out the ammo. And the Yids were taking no chances.

"Hold off, boys," Herzl called out from the top steps. "I've been expecting this visit."

Polanski saddled up beside the boss. "You're supposed to keep me apprised of company coming, Herzl," he grumbled.

"Sorry, kid," Herzl answered, keeping his eye on the pair of luxury vehicles. The boss was pretty much the only one left in the Yid crew who could get away with calling Polanski 'kid' anymore. "This was arranged on the fly. And I wasn't sure they were really coming. Could be good things. Real nachas."

"It's OK, Polanski," Boaz snickered. "This thing's on a need to know basis. Not for pishers."

Was he implying that Herzl had confided in Boaz and not his own head enforcer? Herzl rolled his eyes, but he was polite enough not to make an issue of Boaz' immature pandering. Polanski decided to let it go.

He watched intently as the first ambassadors from Central Station emerged. The bosses were flanked by thick bodyguards. The goons had pale bloated faces and fancy suits. They scanned the crowd of Yids with barely-concealed disdain.

Next came none other than Big Ben, the buck-toothed, mashed-nosed former prize-fighter turned boss. His ample-breasted floozie, Chloe, draped off his arm.

From the second limo, Big Ben's key Central Station ally, the ridiculously mustachioed Francois popped out. Beside him was a red-haired broad Polanski didn't immediately recognize.

Polanski was sure he knew from somewhere.

"Polanski, go get cleaned up," Boaz needled. "You got axle grease on your face."

But Herzl was very serious. "This could be a big deal, kid. I'm going to need you there. Very big deal."

Polanski rubbed the back of his head.

He could feel some pain coming on. As he backed up to head towards the motor pool, he took another quick glance at the woman next to Francois.

Those eyes. Those lips. That face.

She'd dyed her hair, but it was her. When their eyes locked for just an instant, recognition clicked in both of them.

Justine was back.

23
BIG DEAL

"No permanent alliances, just permanent interests," Big Ben reminded everyone around the table. "We're all clear that our interests coincide precisely when it comes to responding to Nasser's latest threats."

Herzl was playing his cards close to his chest. He didn't want to seem too eager. Not that he was dismissive of the opportunity. But the Yids had reason to be suspicious.

"We've been dealing with Nasser's antics for years," Herzl reminded. "Now you want us to help you out? Where were you when we needed you before?"

Francois interjected. "Nasser's move to close off the waterfront and route all his drug shipments through the Upper Eastside is intolerable. With or without you, we won't be locked out."

"Washington doesn't seem to be too worried about it," Herzl suggested, playing devil's advocate. "You couldn't even get him here for this meeting. You think you know something he doesn't?"

"Washington may not want to get involved directly. But he won't try to stop us," Big Ben insisted. "His interests are at stake, too, even if he wants to be coy about this. He's always lecturing the rest of the bosses about keeping the shipping routes open and every gangster getting a bigger slice of a bigger pie. If Nasser shuts down the harbor like he says he's going to, we've got supply problems. Street prices get jacked up and Nasser's got even more cash for Ivan's guns – which are already coming into the Middle Eastside at a big discount, by the way. Not good for you, of course."

Herzl shook his head. "If we make a move behind Washington's back and he doesn't come down hard against any counter-move from the Upper Eastside, it's worse than a wasted effort. We'll be stuck in the middle of a shooting war that maybe we can't get out of. You can always run with your tails between your legs back to Central Station. But we're stuck in this slum with Nasser."

"Washington isn't the only boss in the City," Francois insisted. "He may not want to do anything to upset Ivan. But he'll be forced to come down on our side."

"Listen to what we're telling you, Herzl," Big Ben grumbled. "You know better than anyone the threat that Nasser poses to your operation. He's been making noises about getting even with you boys for years. At the rate Ivan's sending over his guns, Nasser will be ready to take you on sooner than later. Your little dealer in Central Station won't be able to keep up."

Herzl signaled to his top enforcer to make their position clear. "You think you can scare us into making a move," Polanski started. "The days when you could dictate terms around these parts are long gone."

Big Ben and Francois gave each other an uncomfortable look.

Herzl continued. "It's not that we're against the idea of kicking Nasser while he's down. We're tired as all hell of dealing with these rogue Muj running out of the slums and fucking with us. And we're pleased to see that you've finally woken up."

Now his voice took on a somber tone. "But Francois tipped over and left us Yids in the lurch before, when Gruber was running Central Station. And let's face it: you fucked us Yids over when you pulled out of the Middle Eastside. You practically handed that jackass Fariq the keys to the Citadel Hotel."

Big Ben shrugged. "As far as we're concerned, what's in the past is in the past. You may not like that. But that's the way you should look at it too. You Yids have carved out a little turf for yourselves. So now you've got to play ball like the rest of us. If you want to keep your turf, you're going to have to help us."

Herzl was suspicious. But Big Ben wasn't giving up.

"Once our boys are going toe-to-toe with Nasser's crew, you're going to get a lot more from us than we're getting from you. We just need you to poke the bear. We're the ones that have to spear it."

Polanski watched the negotiation with unease. Herzl was still wavering. But Polanski couldn't be sure how much of that was for the benefit of his guests.

After years of working under his boss, he'd gained some insight into Herzl's psyche.

Herzl had achieved something Polanski's father had never really been able to achieve: rock-solid control over a defensible piece of turf. When Herzl got invited for the first time to the United Hotel, he pretty much became a real boss. In theory, he was on par with all the rest of the shlammers who had choked, stabbed and shot their way to the top of their fiefdoms.

But Herzl still had a hangover of an inferiority complex from before; from when the Yids were still hanging on to the margins of power through bribes, cunning and the serial incompetence of their enemies.

Herzl would have to make a move if he wanted to prove himself as a real leader among the other gangsters who owned the City. He'd have to do something brutal. Something risky. A real boss let his big dogs run loose sometimes.

This could be that time.

But he was going to play hard to get a little while longer. "You bastards better have one hell of a plan."

The talks went on long into the night.

24
FAMILY TIES

"You got a name for your kid, yet?" Boaz asked between heaping mouthfuls of kasha. He pointed at Rivkah's swollen belly. His plump wife Zedorah sat next to him, gnawing on a chicken bone.

They were having dinner in Polanski's flat. It was Zev's least favorite day of the week. And he had a lot on his mind while the family talked over mundane matters. He ate in silence while the others carried on.

"Chaim if it's a boy," Rivkah answered. "Zoe if it's a girl."

Boaz frowned. If it was a boy, they were going to name him after Chernik? What a disgrace.

Polanski could read the look on his father-in-law's face. "Not my idea. I liked Chernik and all..."

"It's bad luck," Boaz said, still filling his mouth. "What about Ben?"

Rivkah's face went stern. "It's my decision."

Boaz shrugged. "It's not too late to change your mind."

"I thought you could name him after me, or your grandfather."

"What does it matter what we call the kid?" Zev said. He was bored and annoyed. "Keep it up and we'll give him a Muj name."

An awkward silence settled on the room.

"So, what's the deal with the yokels from Central Station?" Zedorah asked.

Now both Boaz and Polanski went quite. Finally, Rivkah's husband shrugged. "Just business. Nothing to worry about."

Zedorah was suspicious. "They've never bothered coming this way before."

"It's nothing, Boaz added. "Herzl hasn't decided anything yet."

"Decided about what?" Zedorah asked, irritated at the men dancing around her questions.

Polanski shot his father-in-law a hostile look. Boaz wasn't exactly a locked vault when it came to the business if he could feel important shooting his mouth off. And the deal with the boys from Central Station was a tasty piece of news.

"Ma, your plate's done," Polanski interrupted, trying to change the subject. "Rivkah, you want to get your mother some more kasha?"

"It's good," Boaz said. "Not like your mother's recipe, but good."

Polanski looked at Rivkah. They both rolled their eyes.

"You still riding that machine, Zev?"

"It's a motorcycle, pops."

"I know what it is. You should spend more time with your young wife," Boaz said. "Instead of fooling around with that engine all the time. Let the fish take care of it."

"More Yids should get back to doing things," Polanski argued. "Making things. Using their hands. You old Yids don't know how to build shit. That's why this neighborhood never went anywhere until the boys from Central Station came over. Now we get things done."

"You're walking a dangerous line, son-in-law."

"You're jealous since I can sit on my bike without crushing it."

Boaz was unamused. "Respect for your elders, Zev. You never learned that growing up in Central Station."

Polanski's smile dropped. "We were having a nice dinner."

"I hadn't noticed," Boaz grumbled.

Polanski was firm. "I get my work done. The fish get taxed. I keep an eye out for the Muj. What have you got to start up for?"

"Things were different back in the day," Boaz shot back. "Before you got here. This neighborhood was different. Herzl was different. We had an eye on the future. But we respected the past."

110

"Different, how?" Polanski asked.

"Just different."

"What, like you old Yids had to take it in the ass from the Muj and Big Ben so they wouldn't just curb-stomp all of you? Different like that?"

"You Yids from Central Station have an attitude," Boaz said. "The ones who held the ground here don't get the respect they deserve. You weren't here when we had to fight off the Muj and Big Ben at the same time. Life in the Middle Eastside was no cakewalk then. We had no friends then. Everyone schemed against us. But we held this ground for Herzl until you latecomers showed up."

"Fine. We're all very grateful, Boaz. Can I fucking chew my food now?"

"All we're saying is show some respect."

"How about you respect my balls?"

"Zev!" Rivkah shouted. "Don't talk like that," Rivkah hardened.

"It's alright, daughter," Boaz interjected. "Your man has just forgotten to take his medicine today. Or maybe he took too much. You take care of him. You married him."

"Respect," Polanski snarled. "Respect goes both ways, pops. I know what this is really about. I'm not good enough for your princess."

"What, you're just figuring this out now?" Boaz snapped back. "You're no good, Polanski. You're a common shtarke. I don't know what my daughter sees in you. And I don't know what Herzl sees in you, either."

"A man with a good set of balls?" Zev speculated.

"Stop it!" Rivkah shouted at her husband. She was livid. "That's enough."

"Goddamn it," Polanski whispered as he fled the apartment, barely managing to get his boots on before he was out the door.

"Why did you do that? Why do you provoke the boy," Zedorah poked at her husband after Polanski was gone.

"Shut up and eat your kasha," Boaz answered, red-faced and simmering.

111

He was pissed. But he knew he'd overstepped his bounds. It was just in his nature to push buttons.

Meanwhile, Polanski made it down to the garage in record time. Soon he was immersed in the gears of his bike and up to his wrists in axle grease. Everyone else had finished for the day. He was grateful for the solitude.

He was at his station for almost an hour. It was just closing up the engine when a strange yet familiar face with blue eyes poked into the room.

"So it is you," she said. "The eye patch threw me off. So the kid lives."

Polanski turned in her direction. He looked at her. She hadn't really changed. Maybe she was a little softer than before. A little more sophisticated. But her eyes were the same.

"So you're with Francois, now."

"He's already sleeping off two bottles of wine," Justine said.

"You're staying?"

"Herzl's put us up in the new wing of the Citadel. We're staying the night."

"So what do you want with me?" Polanski asked.

"What do you think?" Justine answered. Her eyes sparkled. She hadn't lost that dirty, seductive look that he remembered from long ago.

She could turn it on at will.

"You want to take a ride?" Polanski suggested. "I'll give you a tour of the neighborhood."

"On that thing?"

"Come on," he insisted. "Let's get out of here."

"You sure it's safe?"

"The Muj know who I am. They know my bike. Any putz who takes a shot at me is going to get a face full of lead."

"Sounds like we're going on safari.'

"Something like that," Polanski answered with a mischievous grin.

They hit the road.

25

GETTING TAKEN FOR A RIDE

Justine's fingers dug into Polanski's back through his leather jacket. Her face was nestled into the back of his neck to protect her from the wind.

The motorcycle bound along the road at a fast clip, zipping up and down streets that would have been off limits to the Yids before the turf war.

Now Herzl's gang had a bit of breathing room. Enough to take a ride down a street without getting swiped and shot in an alley. At least in theory.

Polanski's cool nerve was off this night. His thoughts drifted back to back when Justine first knew each other. Back then, she was one of Gruber's molls. Blonde hair, fishnet stockings, a mouth that could inspire the leader himself to attention in an instant.

Of course, Gruber had plenty of attention from the other girls in his employ. But Justine was one of his favorites.

Gruber's attention became increasingly rough as he dominated Central Station. He started treating his girls with an equal measure of brutality.

At first, it was standard slap and tickle kind of treatment most of the molls were used to. Then he started in with the kind of horsing around that left some girls too damaged to make a living from their usual trade. Some wound up dead.

Thanks to the distraction from a steady stream of new girls Gruber picked up from his early successes against his enemies, Justine managed to avoid the worst.

That was when Polanski came into her life.

He was on the run from a team of Gruber's shtarkes that had found his last hideout. Zev climbed a fire escape and broke into Justine's flat.

He was a skinny kid back then. His face was dirty and had an anxious look. But he'd already learned what it took to survive. And part of it had to do with luck. He got lucky that night.

"Stop right there," Polanski heard as he ducked into the room lit by a few candles.

He froze.

Justine was in a tight nightie that showed off her figure down to the most crotch-tightening detail. As he stared down the barrel of her revolver, he thought at least he'd gotten to see this fantasy in his last moments. It was better than getting his clock cleaned by some ordinary shtarke.

The shot didn't come.

Polanski got a good look at this broad. Something was off.

He hadn't noticed at first in the light, but her face was kind of puffy. Her eyes were black. She was like some sort of raccoon woman. And her neck was purple all around.

He couldn't know this was the result of Gruber boxing her in the face and choking her with a belt less than an hour before. That was before penetrating her for a painful but mercifully brief session.

"You're a Yid, aren't you?" Justine asked.

Polanski nodded.

"I didn't know there were any left. How are you not dead?"

"That's the thing about us cockroaches," Polanski said. "It's hard to get every last one."

Her eyes were brutal and cold a moment before. Now they softened. His voice had surprised her.

She tried to look underneath the grime that had was fixed like a mask on his face. "You're just a kid."

Polanski still didn't move. He still wasn't sure if she was going to pull the trigger. "If you're not going to kill me, you got something to eat around here?"

Justine kept the gun on him. "No one saw you come in here?"

"I sure as hell hope not, lady," Polanski answered. "I got five of Gruber's shtarkes out there looking for me. They're not the friendliest bunch. So can you put down the gun?"

"Who are you?"

He wouldn't say. He just stood there.

She waved the gun in his face. "What's your name, kid?"

"Polanski. Zev Polanski."

Her mouth opened and her eyes went wide at the name. Polanski.

"Your father was Herschel. The boss of the Yids from Central Station."

He nodded, wondering what if he'd feel anything once the bullet came into his face.

Gruber had led plenty of his girls into the basement dungeon to take a look at Herschel Polanski in the twenty-eight days it took for him to die in that cage. Every day, new atrocities were committed against him. Dentistry performed without anesthetic. Amputation of fingers and toes, one a day for two weeks. A lead pipe to the knees until they shattered.

Starved. Beaten. Burned.

By the tenth day, the man had utterly lost his mind. He survived only amid a perverse treatment of morphine and first-aid meant to prolong his suffering.

Justine had seen Herschel Polanski on that twenty-eighth day. She'd seen and heard the death rattle that shook the broken man's body in his last moments. All the while, Gruber just stood there chuckling.

She would never forget the sight of it.

Now Zev Polanski stood before her.

His eyes had that same look as his father's before him. A little fear. But mostly, there was a grudging acceptance of his fate.

"Take off your belt," Justine ordered him.

Polanski thought he hadn't heard her right. He did not move.

"Undo your belt. Take off your pants."

Polanski did as he was ordered.

"Sit on the bed." He obeyed again.

115

Justine kept the gun in her right hand pointed at Polanski. With her left hand, she pulled her panties off. She moved to where Polanski was sitting and took in his cock.

"You going to keep that gun pointed at me, lady?" Polanski asked. "It ain't doing much for me."

Justine grunted as he went inside her. "I can tell it doesn't bother you that much."

"Guess not," he answered. He shut up for the rest of their first time together.

That was then.

And now they were riding together on Polanski's motorcycle through the streets of the Middle Eastside. The wind whipped past them. The engine revved up to speed as they twisted and turned on the road.

The memories were still dancing in Polanski's brain as the gunshot cracked.

A bullet ricocheted off the front wheel guard of his motorcycle.

The motorcycle tires screeched as Polanski applied a hard brake, immediately angling the bike to a low profile as he swerved to the right – towards the sound of the gunshot. Justine panicked, digging her nails into his back. He saw a Muj with a pistol running to a stairwell and jumping down to get away.

Polanski went after him.

26
FATHER AND SON

"Hold on," Polanski yelled over the roar of the engine as he gunned it forward. The bike closed the distance instantly. They started bounding down a short flight of steps, hammering the frame as it went down. But the vehicle and its riders held together as they got to the bottom.

A filthy piss-stained alley in the heart of Muj territory opened up before them.

"Are you crazy?" Justine shouted over the engine. "They'll kill us."

Polanski was operating on instinct. He saw the thug with the gun tear into a backyard where nothing grew but ragged weeds and layers of rocks. Trying to escape, he took them to the back door of a detached home next to a big garage and banged on the door.

The weapon fell from the gunman's hand as he panicked. Polanski pulled up to the yard and brought his bike to a halt with a cloud of dust.

"Too late now, friend," he growled, pointing his gun at the shtarke. "Turn around and face me. I don't like to shoot my enemy in the back, but I'll do it."

His failed assassin turned around.

It was a kid, maybe thirteen, fourteen, tops. He was pissing his pants. The left leg of his trousers were dripping.

For a change, Polanski was stuck for what to do.

The back door opened. A frightened older man with a white face and his hands up emerged.

His eyes scanned the situation, from the kid, most likely his son, to the couple on the bike, back to his son, down to the gun on the ground. He immediately sized up the situation.

"You fucking idiot," he shouted at the kid. He instantly transformed from a panicked to furious. He struck the kid in

117

the back of the head. The teenager turned to face his father, only to be struck hard in the chest.

The kid fell and the father kept beating and kicking him mercilessly.

Polanski was a bit at a loss.

He hadn't put down his gun yet. But it seemed less and less likely he'd need to use it.

The father was still shouting. "You steal my gun! You bring the Yids down on us! Fool! What were you thinking?"

The beating continued until Polanski finally intervened. He picked up the dropped weapon and handed it to Justine. "Alright, that's enough," he warned the father and son. They ignored him. The beatdown continued.

"That's enough, I said."

The father looked at Polanski and Justine again, sizing them up. He stopped hitting his kid.

"Get out of my sight," he growled at the kid. The bruised and chastened youth scurried into the house.

The man had a short beard and sunburned skin. He wore clothes that looked like they'd been stitched together last century. He didn't look too tough. Probably just another poor fish, making his way and getting taxed for nothing by Fariq.

But there was something about him. "Alright, let's get this over with," he said without a shred of fear. "Leave him alone. You deal with me."

He put his hands out to his sides pointing at his chest, as if directing Polanski as to where to leave his bullets.

"I'm not gonna kill you, old man," Polanski said. "You're no gangster. Put your hands down. Who are you?"

The man put his hands down. "My name is Abdi. My son is Sayid. Don't kill him, please."

"I'm not going to kill him."

"You're Herzl's enforcer. Polanski."

Polanski's eyebrow went up.

"The eye patch," the old man explained. "Everyone knows who you are."

"You're not one of Fariq's shlammers," Polanski said, sizing up the man. "So what are you doing here?"

118

"You see that garage?" Abdi pointed at it with his thumb. "I fix cars. Bikes, too."

"No kidding."

"That's the F-series, isn't it? Good bike. Hard to get parts, though."

"I need new shocks," Polanski said. "Intake valve's shorting, too."

Abdi nodded. "Come back in a week. I'll get you the parts. No charge. Just labor."

Polanski smiled. "I'll take the parts. But I can do the work myself. You sure you aren't a Yid?"

The Muj gave a nervous smile. "We have to make a living here, too. Fariq's fucking me over. Tax this. Tax that. What did that bastard ever do for me? Or Nasser? This neighborhood's a wreck. At least if we lived near the old Butcher Shop on your street, we'd get something. To keep up appearances."

"Tell you what, Abdi," Polanski said. "I come back, everything works out, I'll have some business for you."

Abdi nodded. "You and your friend. You need somewhere to crash?"

Justine was holding on to Polanski. She was still not quite convinced they were going to be able to get out of the neighborhood alive.

"Maybe," Polanski offered, non-committal. What was this Muj up to?

"That shack you passed just before mine," Abdi said. "It's empty. The owner was one of Fariq's crew that got beat by your side. He died in there."

"What's that got to do with us?"

"No one's every moved in. Place is falling down. But if all you need is a place to be..."

"And why wouldn't you just call down your neighbors on us soon as we leave here?" Justine asked, suspicious.

Abdi shrugged. "You didn't kill my son. That's worth something, isn't it? Besides, he's coming back in a week for the parts. If we're going to kill each other, we can do it then."

Polanski chuckled. "You are a Yid. No doubt about it."

The man kept smiling nervously.

From behind a dirty window of the house, the bruised and bloodied Sayid watched the group of them.

He couldn't stop shaking. Part of it was fear. Mostly, it was restrained fury, not least directed against his father. How could he have humiliated him in this way? Why wasn't he fighting these intruders?

They should have been burying these people, not talking to them. His father was a traitor.

And he was the son of a traitor.

He looked in the mirror of his bathroom. His fear and anger reflected back at him.

One day, he'd be his own man. And he'd get back at them all. He swore it.

27

FUMBLING IN THE DARK

The house was even more desolate than it looked from the outside.

Rodents spied the intruders from the rafters. Everywhere was dust and broken furniture. The only piece that wasn't falling down, the couch in the living room, looked even older than the one in Herzl's office.

The couple half expected to find the old owner's neglected skeleton amidst the ruins. At least the weird neighbors had taken care of that.

"Francois ought to keep a closer eye on you," Polanski said. His eyes trailed down her hair, her shoulders, down her spine, as she paced the room.

"You could say the same thing about your wife," Justine answered. "I hear she's expecting. You're a real tool, Polanski."

"You people from Central Station really keep close tabs on us little people in the Middle Eastside," Polanski said. "You got a measurement on Herzl's cock-length, too?"

"Don't be so fucking crude."

"But you do keep tabs on us," Polanski repeated. "Funny you take an interest after all these years."

"Don't take that line with me," Justine snapped back. "I know where you're from. You're from the same place as me. If you'd grown up half a block down, you might not even be a Yid. Just another one of Gruber's shlammers, dead in the ground, now."

Polanski thought about it. "I don't think I ever fully belonged there, or here."

He searched her face, looking for some sign. "So here's the thing. Can we trust them or what? Herzl's going to come down one way and I don't know what the hell he's going to say."

Justine was suspicious. "You don't think he wants to make a move on Nasser?"

"Maybe he needs a little more convincing," Polanski replied, staring at the couch.

"If you say so," she said, not really committed.

"That's the real reason you came to see me, isn't it? You weren't part of the talks. You could have stayed back in Central Station."

She didn't say anything. She just looked at him, putting her hand on his waist.

"That's it, isn't it," he repeated, looking intently at her.

"Sure," she answered. "What did you think?"

"The boys from Central Station think they can control everything so easy..."

Justine shrugged. "Enough talk. We can do this the easy way or the hard way."

She pointed the gun she'd taken from Sayid at Polanski's chest. "Remember this?"

Polanski looked at her without making a move. "Aren't you gonna ask me to take off my belt first?"

"However you want to play it, Zev." She kept the gun pointed at him.

Polanski grabbed the gun from her and threw it on the ground. He treated her just as roughly, swinging her around and pressing her into the couch.

She gasped as he spread her legs and tore off her panties with one hand. He kissed the back of her neck as he pulled down his jeans and got ready to take her.

She squirmed against him, appreciating the roughness.

It was never going to be a polite reunion.

Not much later, when they'd finished up, she smiled at him through the low darkness in the room. "You're different than before."

Polanski grunted. "So are you."

"I get the feeling maybe you were going to tell Herzl to go in, anyway," Justine said, half a question. "Does he really need persuading?"

Polanski thought about it. "Maybe so. What the hell? Like we need an excuse? Francois knows why you're really here, doesn't he?"

Justine nodded.

"Maybe these fucks from Central Station have us figured out after all."

28
MURDER

There was an apartment block on top of the greasy restaurant chain where Shankmann lived. It was a few blocks from the heart of the Yids' holdings.

But in the dark, the borders of the city took on a more nebulous permeability. Fish kept indoors. But enforcers from all sides tested the true extent of their side's influence.

These things were tested in ways that typically involved sharp objects digging through ribs or shoulder blades. And this would be one of those nights.

Shank noticed there was something wrong when he got home. The lock was busted open. He looked either side on the walkway to his flat. No one around.

He could head back to the Citadel. Call for backup.

He pulled a pistol from his breast pocket. He kicked the door open.

There was no one inside. But a lamp was on. One that he'd turned off when he'd headed to work that afternoon.

"Fuck."

Shank moved in cautiously. A little too slowly, though. Just enough time for the intruder to aim and shoot.

The bullet went into Shank's arm, cracking the bone. Shank dropped his weapon.

A second shot brought him down to his knees.

He raised his head, getting a look at his assassin. A Muj shlammer. Bald. Fat. Not particularly menacing if you saw the guy in broad daylight. But one that could do the job with enough efficiency at point-blank range in bad lighting.

"Shnook," Shank whispered through bleeding teeth. "You won't get away with this. They'll get you."

"They can come and get me," the fat shlammer said. "It doesn't matter, Yid. We've got a few minutes before your friends arrive. Let's make the most of them."

He took a knife out of his pants pocket. The knife was not particularly sharp or expensive or noteworthy in any regard.

But it would do for this job.

Herzl's enforcers heard the gunshots and drew down on the killer hovering over Shank's mutilated form, still breathing shallowly despite the wet work.

And when they killed the assassin with five bullets to the midsection, it wasn't a particularly noteworthy or unique sort of death for that neighborhood. Not really like vengeance.

This was just the sort of thing that went down in the Middle Eastside.

Nothing really out of the ordinary.

Just another couple of dead gangsters in the Middle Eastside.

Unless some people wanted to make something of it.

29
WAR COUNCIL

"Where the hell have you been?" Boaz shouted at Polanski as he got back to the garage. "Herzl's looking all over for you."

Justine had gotten away mere moments before.

"Just took the bike out for a spin, pops," Polanski said. "You're still in a bad mood?"

"Go to Herzl right now," Boaz shouted. "We'll settle up our differences later. What the hell? You smell like you've been at the fish market."

"Fuck off," Polanski grumbled. "I've got to go."

He scrambled through the halls of the Citadel to get to Herzl's office. They were all waiting for him: Herzl, Big Ben and Francois.

And Herzl looked livid.

"What, you haven't heard?" Herzl asked.

Polanski shrugged.

"Fariq's clipped another one of our guys. Nasser says it's this new outfit, the Fedayen gang."

"We know what he's really up to," Francois interjected. "He's testing you Yids. So what are you going to do?"

Big Ben started in. "He's shouting again about closing down the harbor. For security, no less. What a tool."

"Who bought it?" Polanski asked, ignoring the others.

"They got Shankmann," Herzl answered. "Shot him twice. Cut out his tongue and his nose. Poor bastard probably drowned in his own blood."

"They get the son of a bitch that did it?"

"Feldman and Tovey got him. Our boys caught him red-handed. Literally."

"It seems your hand is forced, Herzl," Francois interrupted. "How many of these provocations are you going to take lying down?"

126

"Are you ready to move or what?" Big Ben asked

Herzl still wavered. "Not so fast. We've been dealing with these kinds of ambushes for years before you ever came down to visit. We never had a war from it."

Polanski put his hand on Herzl's shoulder. "This time, we bring the war to them. We ought to do this, boss. The Muj are practically begging for a fight. And we're going to have to go in sometime."

Herzl frowned. "It's risky."

"There's risk in not moving now, too," Polanski said. "We wait and Nasser comes at us next month. And maybe these chumps from Central Station are doing their own thing, no offense. I'm just telling you what I think, boss. You're the one who pulls the cord."

Herzl was maybe the least decisive boss in the whole City. But when his back was to the wall, he knew he had to pick a course and stick with it. So he relented, eyeing his visitors from Central Station carefully. "You say you'll be there for us when we reach the harbor," he said, directing his remarks to the visitors.

"We will be there," Big Ben asserted. "We may have had our differences when we were in the Middle Eastside before, Herzl. But you know we can't let Nasser keep dancing with Ivan. We want to work with you, not against you. We can't let him lock us out of the club."

"You catch his eye for a moment, Herzl," Francois said. "We stab him in the heart."

Herzl shrugged, thinking this is what it meant to be a boss. To go on the attack. To risk it all.

But it was a calculated risk. The Yids couldn't stand on their back foot forever if they wanted to amount to something in the Middle Eastside.

This latest attack was a flimsy pretext, sure. But what about the next time, or the next?

The fight had to come sometime.

It was time to do what was necessary.

"We will do this," Herzl agreed. "You boys better not be fucking with me. Nasser won't go down so easy. We move in two days."

He turned to Polanski. "Get the troops ready. And take a shower," he added with a wink. "You stink like pussy."

30
SERENITY

"Where'd you get to?" Rivkah asked from the bed as Polanski emerged from the bathroom. A cloud of steam flowed away from him.

He was naked except for his eye patch. He came towards her, slinking under the sheets.

"I told you, there was trouble in the tenements," he said. "Shank's dead. They got him."

Rivkah turned on the bedside lamp. She looked at her husband. She looked at his scars from countless brawls and knife fights, most since before she'd ever seen him without clothes.

"They don't stop," he continued. "War. Peace. It's all the same. They don't even give a fuck about turf. Not really, except that we're here. We're not them. So they want us dead."

"I'm sorry I got mad before," Rivkah said.

"Me too, babe," Polanski said. "Me, too."

"What's going to happen?"

"What do you think?"

"Really? Herzl's going to make a move?"

Polanski shrugged. "You know I can't talk about that."

Rivkah frowned. She decided to change the subject. "You and Dad going to patch things up anytime soon?"

Polanski hesitated. "Not that we were best pals way back when. He hated the idea of me marrying you."

"Don't I know it?"

"But Boaz isn't the boss. Herzl is. And I work for him. Talk about respect. How about Boaz respects my place in the organization? How about a little respect this way? I've worked my ass off for these people."

"Forget about my father," Rivkah interjected. "It doesn't matter now."

She put her fingers through his hair, smiling at the feel of it.

Polanski relaxed. "You know I love you, babe." He put his hand on her belly.

"I know."

"You know I'd do anything for you. I'd kill anyone for you."

"That's enough of that talk," she said.

Polanski sighed.

"You want to fuck?" he asked.

"What are you waiting for?"

31
CUTTING LOSSES

The next night, Polanski took his crew over to the old abandoned house on the outskirts of Fariq's slum.

He didn't check in with Abdi. As unexpectedly cordial as their relations were, Polanski figured it was best all around if the Muj didn't know about what went on there.

Polanski had already gone back to the house eight hours before with Boaz. They brought some heavy rolls of insulation. They'd lined a storage room in the decrepit place with the stuff, propping up the dusty rat-chewed mattresses against the walls.

It was a primitive job, but it would do. The room was sound-proofed.

Next came the snatch.

Weissman's spotters had gotten good at nailing down the comings and goings of the shlammers from across the way. He'd even managed to bribe some of the lower level street hoods to rat out their crew.

It wasn't top-level intelligence. But his networks were at least good enough to link the brother of the shtarke who's got Shankmann. And as it happened, he was a regular customer of the Cairo Club, otherwise known as the most horrendous Muj brothel in the Middle Eastside.

Razah was his name. He was a skinny shlammer, with thick afro-style hair and a habit for wearing flashy clothes. He was really easy to pick out of a crowd. And he was a creature of habit; any given afternoon, Razah could be found guarding – well, standing outside, anyway – the Joomla Café at the end of the street.

That's where they'd picked him up. The Muj didn't even have a chance to react. They were in and out. This kind of operation was more about speed and stealth than brute force. Right up Polanski's alley.

The Yids tossed him into the back trunk and made their way back to the old house.

Razah was tied to a chair in front of a table.

Boaz had already slapped him around some. He was bleeding from his lip. And his pants were pulled down to his ankles, mostly just for effect. You want to utterly demoralize a guy, pulling his trousers all the way down is a good way to do it. It's just one of those things you pick up.

Polanski paced the room with a cigarette in one hand. He had a rusty hatchet in the other.

"We got your brother last night, you know," Polanski started. "We shot him."

Razah didn't say anything. He was already sweating. He was afraid.

But he still had a bit of fight left in him. So he kept his mouth shut.

"Word is he was with this new Fedayen gang," Polanski said. "Nasser tells us it's got nothing to do with him. It ain't Fariq's outfit. Got something to do with you, though, right?"

Still silence.

"You know what your brother did to our boy, Shankmann? Cut his nose off. Ears, too. Fucking mess. I mean, good thing he didn't survive, right? What's a guy like that going to do? No face?"

Razah stared at the table.

"Word is you're with Fedayen, too. Which is too bad for you. I mean, if you were with Nasser's crew, maybe... maybe we could cut a deal. Maybe we'd let you go. Nasser ain't no friend of ours, but at least he's got a return address, right?

"But you freelancers. We can't have you guys running around causing trouble."

Boaz slapped Razah in the back of the head. "Not too talkative, eh? Tough guy? Is that it?"

"You got my brother," Razah whispered. "You got no cause to come for me, Yids. I had nothing to do with what went down last night."

Polanski grimaced. "See, that's where you're wrong. You know us Yids ain't too thick on the ground here in the Middle Eastside. We've got a basic problem. Inequality.

132

"We're the minority, see? So for every time someone else fucks with us, we got to roll over eight of your guys just to get even. You know?"

Razah was real quiet now. He was listening.

"But with this new Fedayen gang, we don't know where you guys operate, exactly. We don't have eight guys. We just have you. So we need some help figuring things out, you know? Adding things up.

"Like first of all, we don't think you're a real gang. We think you're still with Fariq or another one of Nasser's outfits. Like I said, it would be better if you were."

Razah had clammed up.

Polanski paced the room. "You married, Razah?"

Silence.

"I'm married. This here's my father in law. Can you believe it? And here's the thing. We don't have a whole lot of time. My wife hates it when I'm late for dinner. Ain't that right, pops?"

Boaz struck Razah in the back again with the palm of his hand. "That's right."

Polanski nodded. "See? If I'm late, my wife's going to be upset. My father-in-law here is going to be upset. So even though I'd like to get to know you a bit better, hear your life story and all that, we just don't have the time. So you're going to have to tell us something."

Polanski gave a signal with his hand and Boaz kicked Razah's chair to the side. His head banged against the concrete floor.

"Hold him," Polanski ordered.

Razah struggled against Boaz. But tied up, he didn't have a chance. Boaz slapped Razah some more to distract the prisoner while Polanski pulled off the man's shoe.

Next, he chopped off three of Razah's toes.

"Fuck," Polanski shouted at Boaz. "I didn't get 'em all. I said hold him!"

"Stop!" Razah screamed as blood ran from his foot.

"What did he say?" Polanski asked. "I didn't hear him. Come on! Hold him! I only got a couple of toes." He drew back for a second strike.

133

"Stop!" Razah pleaded. "I'll talk!"

"No kidding?" Polanski said, sounding a little disappointed. "That was quick."

Boaz shook his head. "That easy? He's not really going to tell us shit. Get the rest of his foot."

"Anything you want to know!" Razah insisted.

Polanski stood up.

His hatchet dripped blood on the floor.

"The Fedayen gang," Polanski started. "Its just Nasser messing with our heads, right?"

"Yes," Razah answered. "Oh, fuck that hurts. It was Fariq's idea."

Polanski shrugged. It figured.

"I'm going to fucking bleed to death," Razah complained.

"You been to the Cairo Club?"

"What?"

Polanski waved the hatchet in Razah's face. "What are you, deaf? I haven't chopped your ears yet. Last time. Have you been to the Cairo Club?"

"Yes, yes. Everyone goes there."

"Many times?"

"Yes, everyone does it."

"No one invited us Yids," Polanski answered. "I hear it's a fun time. Tell you what, Razah. I'm going to give you a chance."

Boaz shook his head. "You've gone soft, Zev."

Polanski ignored him. He focused on Razah.

"I need you to draw me a map. You're going to lay out the place for us. And if this is a really good map, something we can use, then my colleague and I are going to come back here. And we're going to let you go."

"You're lying," Razah said.

Polanski kept talking. "Maybe you can get a doctor to look at that foot."

Razah was quiet again.

"But you fuck with us, if we go there and your map is shit, then we're still going to come back. But we're going to do to you what your brother did to our pal, Shankmann. Only it's

134

going to take three days for you to die. We'll work our way up. You got me?"

Razah stared back. He was scared.

He nodded.

"Alright, then," Polanski said, nodding to Boaz. "Get our new pal some shit to draw with."

"What are we messing with this for?" Boaz growled. "This fool won't help us."

Polanski shook his head and smiled. "Something about this guy I like. Tell you what, Razah. We bandage you up when you're finished. Get you something for that foot."

That's when Razah started working for them.

32

OPENING SHOTS

The next morning, eight men carrying briefcases and duffel bags showed up at the Cairo Club. They arrived on the north-most street in the Middle Eastside in the early morning.

They kept to the shadows before blending into the late night street life. They moved amid the comings and goings of night-owl foot soldiers and their molls.

"Who are you jerks?" the bouncer at the back of the club snarled. His silent partner was equally annoyed. "Rooms are already filled up. You should have got here an hour ago."

"An hour ago, I wasn't close enough to stick a knife in your throat," Polanski answered. He walked right up to his victim, covering his mouth with his left hand. His right jammed an eight-inch blade into the Muj shlammer's neck.

Eban, a new recruit from the Upper Westside, was arguably a bit more crude. He caved in the other shlammer's face with the butt of his pistol.

It was grim, murderous work. But that's war.

The assailants pulled the men into the dark stairwell and finished up their wet work.

Two more guards on the inside were dispatched in equally bloody fashion.

That night, the Yids benefited from an age-old truism that applies to security work. Even if it's your job to stand around and guard stuff, you never actually expect a heavily-armed death squad to show up at your door.

The sentries didn't stand a chance. Their bodies ended up in a hall closet with the other two victims.

Things were still lively in the building, but it wasn't exactly a party. The Cairo Club was the most popular brothel for the Muj in the Middle Eastside. And they liked to give it rough.

Sure, the life of a moll anywhere in the City was never that easy. But it was a different kind of neighborhood than the other boroughs.

In Nasser's hood, the molls got the worst of it.

Some of the high-level enforcers had their own molls they kept in reasonably good shape. They got only an occasional beating to keep them in line.

But most of the molls ended up working places that had more in common with barns than brothels. The girls got beat, used up and disappeared in quick succession.

The sounds of the brutal courtship rituals of this neighborhood were off key to the strangers from Herzl's turf. But they'd have to stay focused on the business at hand.

Luckily for them, Razah's map was accurate enough. They made quick progress after their violent entry.

Polanski's crew went up an elevator to the roof. No guards there. Perfect.

They saw what they were looking for across from their building. The warehouse overlooking the harbor. And a handy way to get over to it.

The warehouse would have been impossible to fight through. Nasser had built it up like a fortress. It overlooked the harbor, from where Nasser controlled the heroin trade and brought in his guns from Ivan.

There had to be at least a couple dozen hard-cracking shlammers in there watching the place at all times.

But the Yids hadn't bothered. There was an easier way, since the Cairo Club wasn't exactly a security priority.

Nasser had missed a huge gaping hole in his defenses. And the Yids were going to make him pay for it.

At one point between the fire escapes on both buildings, the distance was barely eight feet. They could cross that, get to the other side of the square bowl-shaped roof and have a killer view of the harbor. They'd be just out of sight of the Nasser's enforcers below.

Between the two rooftops, they could turn the place into an open shooting gallery.

It was a good plan. But there wasn't any time to lose. They might be discovered at any moment.

137

If their luck held, by the time the sun came up, they'd have everything in place.

The invasion was set to begin.

33
DEATH FROM ABOVE

The Middle Eastside woke up to full-scale war when the sun came up.

The Muj figured something was up when a crew of enforcers watching over a shipment got hit from a long burst of machine gun fire.

Bullets sprayed the deck, mowing down the targets. It was a bloody mess.

A second burst finished off the survivors. Incoming rounds hammered the gas tank of the car where they were unloading their latest shipment of heroin. It exploded in a ball of fire.

It was utter carnage in the harbor.

Simultaneously, on the southeast corner down from the Cairo Club, a trio of enforcers walked out of the Marsh Flats apartment complex. They were on their way to make their rounds for the day.

They heard the burps of gunfire from further west. But mixed into the rest of the morning sounds of cars and shops opening up, it was hard to place the sound. Two of them didn't even notice.

The third cocked his ear, but in the wrong direction.

And two seconds later, their blood was splattered on the pavement.

"Like shooting fish in a barrel," Eban giddily proclaimed from the roof of the warehouse as he fired another burst. The bullets slammed through the window of a high-up apartment to the south. One Muj enforcer had the bad luck to stick his head out. "Except fish are harder to hit."

"Save the big gun for gaggles and crew cars," Polanski warned. "We're going to be up here for a while at least. See those poor bastards in the car at seven 'o' clock? That's what I'm talking about."

Eban let loose with a long burst at the black hearse Nasser liked to use for moving his people around.

The armor plating on the sides wasn't good enough to keep out 7.62 caliber rounds. In any event, there wasn't really any protection to be had from this angle. The Yids were shooting down into the street.

Casualties mounted fast. Three-dozen corpses later, the Muj had located the Yids on top of the harbor-front warehouse and the Cairo Club.

They instantly realized Herzl's goons had pretty much total control from where they were perched, looking down to at least four blocks to the south.

Muj shlammers couldn't even get out into the road to drag back the bodies. Anything that moved in the streets didn't keep moving for long.

Nasser was going to have a very bad morning. The counter-attacks he launched all failed with bloody results.

A crew of six of Nasser's hand-picked enforcers went down first. They got crushed in the elevator of the Cairo Club when the rigged cable snapped on the fifth floor.

Another team on the stairs up to the roof ended up dead from a simple tripwire and a grenade hanging on a string.

A web of booby traps that had taken the Yids about thirty minutes to set up would take the Muj the better part of a day to dismantle.

The guards at the warehouse didn't have any better luck. They got up on the fire escape at the warehouse to go up to the roof. The weight of the four unfortunate thugs who clambered up the railings was enough to loosen the framework Eban had sabotaged.

The whole upper fire escape structure collapsed. The men tumbled seven stories to the pavement.

Their skulls popped on contact like ripe watermelons.

About fifty Muj down and no casualties to the Yids, yet. It was turning out to be a good morning for Herzl's gang.

Keeping Nasser's waves of fighters and weapons at bay was only the first part of the plan. The Yid spotters confirmed that the streets on Nasser's turf had emptied out. No one was moving.

The anvil was in place. Now it was time for the hammer to strike.

34
CRASH

Nasser was getting sick of having his ass handed to him.

He'd already repressed all memory of his authorization for putting that ridiculous Fedayen gang into action. And of course, his threats to close off the harbor to all traffic except himself and his client in the Upper Eastside could not have set off this chaos. His provocations and ultimatums could not possibly be seen as... provocations and ultimatums.

No, blame was to be found in an old familiar culprit.

It always came down to Fariq. That dope had gotten them into the shit in the first place, with that first abortion of a war. He'd lost an entire street to the Yids that time for his trouble. And now his cousin's dreams of reflected glory had once more sabotaged his operations.

This "Fedayen gang" ruse that was supposed to wear down the Yids one back-alley stabbing at a time had set off a full-blown turf war. It was a war he should have been able to fight decisively thanks to Ivan's generous supplies of firepower.

But now a single Yid street crew was holed up on his roofs, keeping the north side of the borough locked down. All of his guns, all of his henchmen on these streets had to sit tight. Nothing got in or out.

And the enemy was pressing their advantage.

"The Yids are coming at us with cars, grenades, machine guns..." Bashir, a street-crew captain from the next block over complained.

He was practically hysterical.

"We've got all those things, too," Nasser growled. "And we outnumber them eight to one. What the hell are you waiting for? Hit them!"

142

Bashir shook his head. "We can't close in. We're pinned down out there. They're taking us out one building at a time."

Right at that very moment, Boaz had just rammed his car through the window of a Muj hangout on Eighty-fourth Street. The reinforced bumper and souped-up engine made the vehicle an efficient tool for clearing buildings.

Boaz' accomplices in the back sprayed the opened-up lobby with lead through the tops of the windows. They took down three of the Muj gunmen. Their retaliatory fire just bounced off the bulletproof hood.

Boaz emerged from the driver's seat as he had done several times this morning, cradling his shotgun.

The one he'd actually managed to run over was still conscious, though gasping for air. He'd probably busted some ribs.

Boaz shrugged and put the shotgun into his shoulder. There was a flash from his barrel as the top of the gangster's head disappeared into a fine red mist.

"How about the other two?" Boaz asked.

"This one's still breathing," another fat shlammer named Neumann, originally from the Upper Westside, called out from the right-hand corner.

He fired two shots with a magnum pistol. "Oops. Not anymore."

"Worziawsky!" Boaz shouted. "Any more in the back?"

"It's clear," the third shlammer called back. "No one got out."

"Alright, then. Get back in the car. We got a time-table to meet."

Meanwhile, Nasser had run out of patience with his shlammers. "I don't care what you have to do," he ordered Omar. Bashir's bullet-riddled corpse littered a corner of the boss' office. "Take out those bastards on the roof!"

"We've tried," Omar pleaded, very much aware of Bashir's body a few steps to the left. "We've lost six street crews to those Yids. We can't get up there."

Nasser considered shooting Omar. He considered it very hard.

143

But perhaps it wasn't his fault he was a complete idiot. So many of his shlammers were.

He made a mental note for all of his crew bosses to stop punching the younger low-performing gangsters in the head.

"This is what you're going to do," Nasser ordered through gritted teeth. "In the basement of the Cairo Club, there is a large crate of plastic explosives. I've been storing them next to the cages. You know, the ones where we keep the fresh meat."

Omar nodded.

"Take my personal armored car. The Yids would need a bazooka to get through the hull. Take two men with you. When you get there, place the charges. There is enough bang-bang there to bring down the building."

"Er, boss, there are still many of our own trapped in there," Omar checked. "As soon as they poke their noses outside, the Yids' guns will get them."

Nasser shrugged. "They are not much good to me anyway if they don't fight."

"But the girls..."

"If you tell anyone there, they'll all try to leave at once. The Yids on the roof are cunning. They may figure out something is up. And I don't want them to escape. So don't give them a clue."

Omar nodded.

"Get in, set the bombs, get out," Nasser explained. "Can I count on you or should I call in a gangster who actually works for me?" Nasser said, pointing his gun at Omar from his desk.

He was smiling, but not in a friendly way.

"I'll take care of it boss," Omar said.

He'd never set a bomb in his life. But he did want to keep breathing.

35

FALLING DOWN

The helicopters showed up at four 'o' clock in the afternoon. They came in over the water and veered towards the rooftops where the Yids had taken up residence.

One of the chopper doors slid open and one of Big Ben's buck-toothed fancy boys appeared with a megaphone. He blared out at them in a voice that carried down to the streets below. It was meant to. They were putting on a show.

"Hey you assholes on the roof! Put your weapons down! Big Ben says your war is over. Our forces are here to separate both sides." There was a shlammer sitting behind a coaxial machine gun next to the guy with the megaphone. He made the threat seem genuine enough.

Polanski stepped back from his weapon. He motioned for the rest of his crew to do the same. "Guess we better do what they say, boys."

"We're coming in," the shlammer on the loudspeaker bellowed. "Any hostile act by your side will be met with extreme prejudice."

Herzl's lieutenant lit a cigarette. He waved at them as they came in.

The crew stayed low as the first helicopter descended onto the roof. The second helicopter did the same on the roof of the Cairo Club. The pilots cut the engines at about the same time.

Big Ben's rep slid down to the roof of the warehouse.

"About time you got here," Polanski said with a grin. "There's no shitter on this roof. We all got to take care of business."

"Think you gents can hold it 'til we drop you off?" said the man with the megaphone. He introduced himself as Basil.

"You better hope so," Polanski said. "Could get unpleasant."

"Fair enough," Basil replied with a smirk. The Yids started to pile themselves and their weapons into the helicopter. "How did you boys make out up here?"

"Not much action since this morning," Polanski said with a shrug. "I see Boaz' crew are causing a ruckus in the streets. But this neighborhoods been locked tight since the Muj figured out what was happening."

"Do you think our friend Nasser will see through our little charade?" Basil asked.

"I guarantee he already has," Polanski said with a shrug. "Nasser's operation's always been lousy with dumb shlammers. But he isn't totally fucking stupid. Your boss and Francois can tell him and the rest of the City any story you like. He'll know we were in this together."

"Then why did your boss agree to go along with this charade?" Basil asked, putting a bowler hat on to keep out the wind.

"What makes you think he really had to be convinced?" Polanski shot back with a grin. "So where are your boys at?"

"Right this moment?" Basil answered. "Our street crews have already crossed into the Middle Eastside. You see those boats down there? Big Ben's really sending in the cavalry for this one."

Their helicopter had just gotten off the roof of the warehouse. The other bird was still on the roof of the Cairo Club, just a few seconds from taking off after them, when that building collapsed.

In the basement, Omar had gone and blown himself up in the process of rigging the explosives.

Along with himself, he also exploded or buried alive forty-three Muj. But the bomb did what Nasser wanted it to do.

The four Yids on the roof, a pilot from Central Station and the helicopter came crashing down in a burst of flame and smoke and dust.

The force of the explosion warped the air, causing Basil's helicopter to very nearly crash into a five-storey tower. The pilot managed to bank up right at the last instant.

146

"Fuck fuck fuck fuck fuck!" Polanski yelled. He was apoplectic at the sight of the disaster. "Just another ten seconds. Five seconds. Fuck them. Fuck them."

Basil shook his head. "If it's any consolation, my friend, our boys are about to give Nasser the shit-kicking of his life."

Polanski frowned. "That's some consolation."

"But before we leave, would you like to take a turn at the machine gun? Seems like the fireworks from the explosion has brought the Muj out from under."

Polanski looked back at Basil. He looked at him very hard.

Then he looked down to see that the Muj were indeed cautiously stepping into the street to see what had become of the Cairo Club.

Now Polanski let out just the barest hint of a grin. "You really know how to cheer a guy up."

Polanski fired off a long burst with the machine gun. The Muj scattered again as the rounds hit the pavement.

36
THE HAMMER FALLS

The past twelve hours had been rought for Nasser's forces in the Middle Eastside. But it was about to get a lot worse.

Big Ben and Francois were thirsty for action. And they were about to take it all out on Nasser.

The crews from Central Station had a good thing going on their own turf. Regardless of Nasser and Ivan's business boycott, there was plenty of dough to be made. They had all kinds of scams going. It was all busting, thanks to some creative underwriting from the Upper Westside (mostly to keep Ivan's dirty fingers out of there).

But gangsters that have it too get start turning into fish. And Big Ben and Francois knew it.

Their boys hadn't had a decent rumble since they'd finally beat Gruber's operation. And they could hardly take the credit for the final victory. To this day, Washington and Ivan both ran their own extensive operations in Central Station.

So now was the time to get their crews back in action. They had to show the rest of the City that they were still in control of their destiny. And that meant stomping all over their old stomping grounds.

Herzl's crews had been content to smash and grab. They moved and flowed around the strong points. The horde from Central Station went straight for Nasser's pressure points.

The harbor was first; after all, that was technically the key to the operation. Big Ben's shtarkes moved in. Francois' enforcers fought their way into the warehouse.

Now the fighting wasn't just with pistols, automatics and the odd machine gun anymore. These shtarkes had flamethrowers; real armored cars with mounted artillery; rocket launchers. The works.

For the next three hours, Nasser's turf was a bloodbath. His crews for the first three north blocks got smashed to smithereens.

Once the invaders got outside of their three-block landing zone, the going got harder for the invaders. Nasser could hit back with heavy weapons of his own.

A pair of Big Ben's armored cars went up in a fireball. A mortar round hit precisely in the center of a gaggle of Big Ben's forces. It turned them into chunks of meat. Machine guns dueled from street corners, raking goons from both sides.

But Nasser's forces couldn't hold the line. They pulled back further. Fires spread now between buildings. And Nasser's few remaining cars gunned it southward for the boss' main stronghold.

In the basement of that bunker, Nasser sweated and stared at the wall, alone. He looked at the gun on his desk. And he tried to look at something else.

It was looking very much like the end for Nasser and his gang.

But on the verge of a game-changing debacle in the Middle Eastside, the fighting was about to come to an abrupt halt.

37

UNFINISHED BUSINESS

Justine caught Polanski as he came down from his flat into the garage. He'd been back for a few hours and now he was coming back up for air.

"Shouldn't you be in there with your boss planning all sorts of mischief?" Justine asked.

"Herzl's busy. There's something going on now he's got to deal with. Rivkah's tending to the wounded in the basement. No one applies a tourniquet better. She's going to be occupied for a while."

"So we've got some time."

"You're crazy."

"You think so?"

"Maybe we both are," Polanski acknowledged. "But we can't keep this up.

"Look, I'm just glad you made it back in one piece."

"Turned out I had a fifty-fifty shot," Polanski said. "The other fifty per cent weren't so lucky."

"You going to be alright, Zev?"

"I'll be fine. What are you still doing here, anyway? I thought you'd be back in Central Station by now."

"Francois thought it would be better for me to stick around here. But to tell the truth, there's been nothing for me to do since you left. So where are you headed on that bike?"

Polanski grinned. "Look, I was serious. We can't mess around like before. Not anymore. I've just got some unfinished business to take care of."

"How about I come with you?"

"I told you its business."

"I'm sure it's nothing I haven't seen before, Zev," Justine insisted. "Sure you don't want me along? Last time, you nearly got clipped. Maybe I'm your good luck charm."

Polanski considered it as he crouched on his motorcycle. He checked around, searching the shadows for eavesdroppers. No one could see them leave together.

"Alright, hop on," he said. "Make it quick. And I'm serious. No funny business."

"Spoil sport."

Soon they were zipping away from the Citadel.

These streets were quiet. All of Fariq's decent foot-soldiers had joined the fight just four blocks west. They were getting shit-canned just the same as the rest of Nasser's enforcers.

The Butcher's Shop was still chock-a-block with shtarkes; the Yids thought Fariq's boys would rather see the rest of Nasser's streets get rolled up than lose that one building. The Asqua Club was Fariq's crown jewel; his last tie to any kind of power since he'd got beat years back.

The Yids would have to go in with tanks to take it away from the Muj.

But the rest of the turf bordering the Yids' holdings was actually pretty quiet. On the back-routes to the broke-down hovel near Abdi's place, the path was as safe as anywhere a Yid was likely to go in the City.

They entered the dusty ghost of a home once again. Memories of their rendezvous a few nights ago were still fresh in their mind. "You always were a romantic, kid," Justine said.

She started undoing the buttons on his shirt, but he pushed her away. "I told you, I got business here."

"I thought that was just a line to get away from me. Or to get you away from your wife."

"No, really. Take a seat."

Justine eyed the furniture where they'd fucked just a few nights before. It was a total disaster. She laughed. "I'll stand."

"Suit yourself."

"What are you doing with that?" she asked, a chill suddenly going up her spine as he picked up the hatchet propped nonchalantly in front of a closet door.

There was bad light from the hanging light bulb in the center of the room. But she could tell the tool was stained with something sticky. Something rusty-colored.

"I suggest you get back, darling," Polanski said. "This could get rough. This is my business, now."

He unlocked the bolt and kicked open the door.

It was dark inside. He flipped a switch.

Razah was still there. He was still tied up. But he was awake.

He stared at his captor with sunken eyes that radiated hate.

"How's the foot," Polanski asked.

He said nothing.

"What? You giving me the silent treatment? I'm going to let you go, you know. Can you walk on it?"

Razah stared. "I can't feel it."

"That's too bad."

"Can't feel my leg from the knee down. You fucking Yid savage."

Polanski thought about it. "Look, I'm here to let you go. So go easy on the 'Yid savage' stuff. You might hurt my feelings."

"You think you can fool me?" Razah snarled. "You're going to kill me."

"No, Razah, listen to what I'm telling you," Polanski answered calmly. "I'm a man of my word. You drew a map for me. And it worked pretty well. Thanks to you, there's about a hundred of your buddies that aren't breathing now. I know this place was sound-proofed, but maybe you heard some of the bang-bang?"

"Fuck you," Razah answered through gritted teeth. He was pale. Sick. Probably suffering from gangrene in his foot.

But he was defiant. The way he figured it, he had nothing to lose.

"Well, what's it going to be, Razah?" Polanski asked. "The door's open. I'm not going to stop you."

"You're going to kill me," Razah insisted. "You'll pretend to let me go. Then you'll wait until my back is turned and you're going to kill me."

152

Polanski shrugged. "Fuck, Razah. If I wanted to kill you, I would have just done it. But I'm tired of this. You know what? You're fucking boring."

"How awful for you, Yid."

Polanski frowned. "I just thought of something."

Razah stared. He waited for Polanski to make a move.

"I got a deal for you, Razah. I'm going to give you this hatchet, see? I'm going to give it to you. You can fight me for your freedom. Get some of your honour back."

"You've got a gun."

"No self-respecting Yid thug would go without."

"I can't do it with a hatchet," Razah said, his eyes still searching, darting at Polanski's face. "I can't get to you... on one foot. You'll shoot me."

"So it's not fair, is what you're telling me"

"You'll kill me."

"You know, Razah?" Polanski said, staring back at him. "I'm a fair man. You're right. You're on one leg. Besides, axe versus gun? The gun wins every time. Sure, I should have known that."

Silence.

"I'm going to give you my gun, Razah," Polanski said.

Justine heard what was happening. "What are you doing in there? This is insane."

"I'm working, darling," Polanski said. "I can't deal with you right now, see? This is between me and my friend Razah, here.

"Alright, buddy. Here's the deal. You get the gun. I stick with the hatchet. You kill me, you get to walk out of here. Well, crawl, maybe. You're not going to get a better deal."

Razah agreed. "Give me the gun, Yid."

"Don't do this!" Justine screamed. "Stop it!"

Polanski frowned. He pulled his pistol out of his pocket and tossed it to Razah.

It clattered to the floor in front of him.

"Do it," Polanski ordered.

Razah picked up the gun. He pointed it at Polanski.

And he pulled the trigger.

Click.

153

Click. Click. Click. Click.

Polanski walked straight up to Razah. He raised up that hatchet and drove it straight down into the middle of Razah's skull.

Blood splattered up on his face.

He drove it down again. And again.

Justine stood in the doorway. "You knew," she stuttered. "You knew the gun wasn't loaded."

Polanski turned to face her. "You know the crazy thing?"

She didn't answer.

"I really was going to just let him leave. That was some map. It was like a work of art or something. Like architecture blueprints. And the shnook sketched it with three of his toes on the other side of the room. That's something."

He dropped the hatchet and walked towards her.

She didn't try to run. She put up a hand on his forehead, wiping away the blood.

That's when Boaz walked in the front door of the old house. He was armed with a shotgun. And he did not have a happy expression on his face.

"What is going on here? What the fuck are you two doing here?"

Justine drew away from Polanski. She retreated to the wall. Polanski pointed into the closet. "I had to take care of our prisoner," he said.

"That's why I came here," Boaz said.

"I know," Polanski said. "That's why I had to get here first."

Boaz looked into the closet. "Good work. You could have waited."

He came out of the closet and saw Justine. "So, what are you doing here?"

He looked back at Polanski. Then back to Justine.

Boaz' face darkened. "You lousy lying sack of shit," he growled at Polanski. "My only daughter..."

He leveled his shotgun at his son-in-law.

"It's not what you think," Polanski pleaded.

"My only daughter," Boaz repeated. His face had darkened almost black. His eyes were filled with rage.

Polanski slammed his right hand against the barrel. He knocked it to the side as it fired. His fist slammed Boaz in the jaw.

It had absolutely no effect. Boaz was pumped with rage.

The old mountain of a man grabbed Polanski's arm and twisted it, forcing him down. He kept twisting as Polanski squirmed. In another moment, the bone would snap.

Justine brought down the hatchet on the centre of Boaz' back. Boaz screamed and let go of Polanski. He slammed his meaty shoulder into her.

She banged against the wall and slumped to the floor.

But by the time Boaz turned back to Polanski, the shotgun barrel was pointed at his own chest.

Polanski pulled the trigger.

Boaz got a full load at point-blank range. He slumped to the floor.

Justine was still down. She was woozy. "Get up, babe," Polanski urged. She slumped back to the floor, still dizzy.

Polanski heard footsteps crunching on the gravel outside the house. His eyes narrowed.

A shadow appeared on the porch. Then a silhouette appeared in the doorway.

Polanski swung the shotgun like a baseball bat. The stock smashed into man's head, cracking the skull.

The body fell outside.

Polanski crouched over the body. It was the neighbor. He'd been drawn in by the noise.

He wasn't breathing.

"Fuck," Polanski cursed under his breath.

He looked over at Abdi's house across the way. He couldn't see Sayid staring back at him from the darkness, highlighted under the moonlight. But he knew someone had seen him.

"We've got to go, babe," Polanski urged Justine. She stumbled out of the shack and he helped her on to his bike. They rode off into the night as Sayid came to hover over the body of his dead father.

155

The son stood there for a very long time.
Then he went into the old broken-down house.

38
CEASEFIRE

The party was in full swing. Herzl, Big Ben and Francois celebrated on the roof of the Citadel Hotel, enjoying the view of the Middle Eastside.

The scene was practically apocalyptic.

Nasser's turf was ablaze. Smoke hovered over his territory to the southwest. Gunfire ripped the night.

For those present, this was a good thing.

The champagne poured. The visiting bosses had brought delicacies and cigars from Central Station.

The host was red-faced with enthusiasm. He'd never felt quite this high. It was liberating.

But the good times would not last.

"What's that?" he said, staring up at the dot of an aircraft making its way from the north. "You boys bringing more champagne?"

Big Ben and Francois were chuckling. And then, suddenly, they stopped laughing. They got awful quiet.

They didn't say anything. But Herzl got the distinct impression that they seemed nervous.

And that made him nervous.

When they realized who owned the bird heading their way, they all felt a shudder of dread.

Washington's big helicopter swooped in and descended to the roof of the Citadel Hotel. It blew the fragile rooftop furniture over. The wine spilled on the tarmac.

The most powerful boss in the City got out. He was flanked by two no-nonsense shtarkes made of stone. They openly cradled light machine guns in their thick arms.

The waiting trio said nothing as the helicopter's engine whined down. They could see from Washington's face that the man was capable of just about anything. Intuitively, their own faces became masks with which to suck up.

Washington stared hard at them.

"I should throw all three of you off the roof right now," he started. "You have no idea of the shitstorm you've set off."

"We thought... We thought you'd be pleased," Big Ben started. "Nasser was cutting you out, too. He was getting too close to Ivan."

Washington cut him off. "Let me tell you how close Ivan is getting. He's got half of his troops lined up about six blocks from here. They're ready to roll on through the Middle Eastside. They'll probably stop in and pay you a visit, first, Herzl. Then they're going to wrap up the rest of this neighborhood and plant a big fucking flag.

"Now, the other half of his forces are bunched up right on the outskirts of Central Station. He could invade at any time. Your forces are playing cowboys with Nasser? You've left your home turf wide open."

"Ivan wouldn't dare," Francois said.

"Francois, the only thing that's holding him back right now is me. Like always, let's face it. And I've got to tell you, I'm sorely tempted to give him the green light."

"But why would he make a move now?" Big Ben asked.

"Ivan thinks I put you boys up to this. Of course he does. Why wouldn't he? You have so thoroughly fucked me over this time."

"You want us to pull our forces back," Herzl said.

"Bing! The Yid gets it on the first try. Damn you, Herzl, I thought you were smarter than this. Hooking up with these has-beens? You remember I made you, Herzl? I saw you. I recognized you. The rest of the bosses, they weren't so sure about even letting you into our club. I vouched for you. And this is how you repay me."

Herzl was chastened. He was pretty sure if he talked back now, he'd be on the receiving end of a semi-automatic. He kept his lips zipped.

"All of you are pulling out right now. Otherwise, Ivan's foot-soldiers will be shoving their pistols in your mouths in about half an hour."

"Our gangs have not fought for nothing," Francois insisted. "By morning, Nasser will be gone. You do not own us, Washington. We can do this, whether you approve or not."

The big man from the Upper Westside showed no emotion. He merely nodded to one of his statuesque guards.

The mammoth scooped Francois up by the armpits, rushed him over to the rooftop ledge and flipped him upside down like he was playing with a rag doll.

The enforcer dangled the lesser boss by his right ankle. There was nothing else between him and the pavement many stories below.

Washington edged over next to the dangling Francois. "Listen up and listen good, my friend," Washington started. There was a lethal undercurrent to his tone. "I do own you. I own you all. And if I choose to let you go, you will fall."

"Let me down!" Francois pleaded.

"You sure about that?" Washington asked with a smirk. Francois realized his poor choice of words as Washington's shlammer's grip loosened just the tiniest bit.

He begged the boss of bosses not to kill him.

"Put that fucker back on the roof, Sal," Washington said. "We still need him to tell his boys to pull back."

Francois fell in a heap on the roof. Big Ben and Herzl watched in awe.

"Well," Washington interrupted, bringing them back to life. "Unless you all want to end up on the pavement, you'd best get to it."

In five minutes all went quiet in the Middle Eastside. The gunfire stopped, at least from one direction.

A rapid withdrawal was about to begin, ordered by the three formerly victorious bosses. The illusion of their free will was robbed from them.

Not much later, Big Ben and Francois had already left the scene. But Herzl remained on the roof with Washington. "What a colossal clusterfuck, Herzl," he started. "You really let me down, pal."

Herzl didn't quite know what to say. He was older than Washington by some years. But now he felt like a scolded schoolchild.

As a boss with his own turf, he ought to have felt enraged at Washington's presumption.

But Herzl had always had a pragmatic and intuitive side. He knew how things really worked. And he knew he'd disappointed the man.

"So what do you think is going to happen, Washington?"

The boss of the Upper Westside shrugged. "If we're lucky, Ivan will take the hint. He'll pull back. We all end up with egg on our faces.

"But we don't quite go back to the status quo. You still come out ahead. Nasser's got his clock cleaned. He'll build up again in time. But you bought yourself some breathing space. Fact is, if I were you, I would have done the same thing. That's what pisses me off about all of this."

"I respect you, Washington," Herzl said. "Don't let anyone tell you different. But what do you want for this place? What do you want from us?"

"So long as Ivan's got his dirty fingers in this place, what I want doesn't matter," Washington answered. "I can't operate like I want. But long term. That's what matters."

"I do like that about you, Herzl. You're always thinking about the future. Planning. Building. You've got enemies to the right and left. No decent rackets the rest of us would bother horning in on. But you've established yourself. That kind of gumption gets noticed."

"Look, push comes to shove, you know you've got me in your corner. If you ask for it. But then I'm your boss. You don't need that. I don't want that. And no one else wants it either."

"Maybe so, Washington," Herzl said. "It doesn't make my job easier."

"What, are you looking for sympathy?"

"Just saying. In some ways, it was easier before when we let others run protection for us. But it's no way to be in this City. We've learned that lesson the hard way."

Washington smiled. "You worry too much. You want to know my secret, Herzl? You want to know how I got to where I am today? It's something those bozos from Central Station

160

forgot a long time ago. And it's the reason Ivan's never going to be anything but second-class compared to me. And it's why you've got a shot at making a go of things here."

"Lay it on me, then," Herzl said. He looked amused.

"Take care of the little fish. Take care of your people. Let 'em run free and do what they do best. The big picture takes care of itself."

Herzl thought about it. "It's that easy, huh?"

"Or you could go Ivan's way. Shoot all of your under-performers and hope the rest shape up," Washington said. "But I don't think you've got enough Yids to spare."

"Maybe I'll go your way, then."

"Glad to hear it," Washington replied. "And here's to a few more years of peace in this place, at least until Nasser gets his balls back again. Care to join me in a cigar, Herzl?"

"I'd be honoured, Mr. Washington."

"To peace. And all that comes with it."

39

RECONCILIATION

Rivka was waiting at the empty dining table when Polanski walked in.

"Zev!" she shouted and sprang to her feet. "Where have you been? The others were already back for hours."

He didn't say anything. His face was still splattered with blood that trailed into his eye patch. His right eye looked out with a dead sort of stare.

Rivkah knew something was wrong.

She came close to him. She saw the blood. His skin was pasty.

He reeked of sweat and gun smoke.

"Where have you been?"

"I'm sorry I'm late, Rivkah," he whispered. "Real sorry." He seemed different. Vulnerable, like she hadn't seen him in a long, long time. Not since the day he'd lost his eye.

"It's alright, Zev," Rivkah said. "It's alright."

He stopped inches from her. He couldn't bring himself to hold her.

She stepped into him, her head tucked under his chin. "Listen," she said. "The guns have stopped."

She could hear him breathing, slowly. But he still would not speak.

"Tell me," Rivkah asked again, more gently this time. "Where have you been?"

"I'm sorry, Rivkah," Polanski answered. "Your father. He is dead."

"Dead?"

"But they said the fighting was over. And he came back..."

"It happened an hour ago," Polanski said. "We had to go to Muj territory for one last job."

"You saw it happen?"

Polanski nodded.

"Damn them," Rivkah said.

They stood there a while in the living room.

"Rivkah."

"Yes, Zev."

"You know I would do anything for you. For our child."

"I know that," she said. Until that moment, she'd never truly believed that. But now, she could feel it.

After a few more minutes, she pulled away, reluctantly. "I must tell my mother."

Polanski nodded. "Go to her now. I'll be here."

Rivkah left. Polanski still stood there a long while.

He pulled off his eye-patch over where his left eye had once been. Even now, it hurt really bad. His head was throbbing. He held his hand over the spot. The pain was worse than it had been in ages.

But he decided he would not need his drugs anymore.

It was better to live with the pain. So he just stood there and took it all in.

PART 3
1967

40
CHANGES

The little garden patio where Herzl liked to take his coffee in the middle of the afternoon was a sort of a refuge. He liked it better than the dusty sanctuary of his old office. He even did some gardening out here now. Tomato plants. Cucumbers. Flowers. Some of his gangsters thought he'd gone a bit soft in his old age. But he just liked the way things looked now.

Beefy guards with ironed shirts and automatic weapons patrolled the courtyard. Beside them, tall trees had taken root in this place. And a quaint little iron gate led out on to the street. All of the greenery and rustic style in this place almost made the view of Fariq's slum bearable.

The ground had shifted in the Middle Eastside. In the last war, the aggressors were forced to retreat back to their starting lines. The fury wrought on Nasser's turf had been repaired with a patchwork job that showcased the waste and corruption of their enemies. The Muj holdings across the street were defined by backwardness and decay.

Once more, a power balance had been struck. The Yids were still confined in a relatively tiny holding in the Middle Eastside. And as before, Nasser had cultivated ties with Ivan to rebuild his strength. But deterrence was now in play. Incidents along the boundaries of their territories were rare.

Herzl had made full use of the meager time and space he'd been given. He took care of his fish. The gang's rackets made few predations upon their legitimate interests. He sunk real cash into developing the place.

The plants in the courtyard were only the smallest sign. A modest measure of tranquility and prosperity had come to this part of the Middle Eastside.

To be sure, Herzl's enforcers had not gone soft in the meantime. The changes in the neighborhood only gave them greater cause to keep up their regimen. Guns still ruled here. But there was more to protect.

More of the Yids of the Upper Westside and even some decent enforcers from Ivan's holdings had made their way here. Herzl had warmly welcomed these fresh recruits. And thanks to the modest gains of the wars, he had more apartments to put them in.

As the Yids' domain built up and the buildings took on a sort of comfortable stone hue shaded by trees and the renovations of the fish, Fariq's slums had fallen into utter chaos.

Security was still an overriding concern for the Yids. Immediately to the Citadel's front and west flank, the Muj were restive.

The false-flag Fedayen gang had been an amateurish ruse before. But now many real tribal groupings had broken out amongst the Muj. Was Fariq in charge of them? Was Nasser? The top Muj gangster boss seemed to have washed his hands of his cousin's chaotic street crews.

Total neglect had made virtual enemies of Fariq, these new gangsters and their formal leader. Though Nasser claimed to champion their cause, he could no more walk in some of the slums than Herzl could.

Those awful dens of horror-show gangsterism had become dense hives of dark deeds. None outside them ever ventured into these warrens.

Herzl was taking in the dismal view from the courtyard when Polanski arrived for their daily session. As usual, he had a singular focused look to him. He was all business these days.

Years ago, Herzl's top enforcer had traded in his flack jackets and leather motorcycle gear for more upscale attire. Now he wore a formal black suit modeled on Herzl's style. He looked almost dashing. Herzl smiled at the sight.

Polanski sat down in his usual spot. Soon, Weissman joined them at the table. A waiter instantly came over to pour them hot black coffee.

"So what's going on in the neighborhood?" Herzl asked.

"Two of Fariq's fish ended up shot dead in an alley last night about a block from us," Polanski reported. "No confirmation yet on who did it. Too many little bosses running their own operations. Everything's still out of control down there."

"No spillover to us?" Herzl asked.

"None yet," Polanski said. "We're clear. The Muj are really fucking themselves over."

"So what else is new? Anything else?"

"Big shipment from Ivan into the harbor early this morning. A whack of AK-47 rifles and two crates of ammunition. Mortar rounds. Something that looked like it might be an artillery piece."

"Excellent," Herzl said with a shrug. "The putz must have a gun in every spare closet by now. You'd think he could dole out some cash to fix up his borough. Maybe fill in some potholes?"

"He's got guns, but his shlammers are still next to worthless," Polanski said. "The meshugah loses two wars and doesn't learn a thing."

"It's good for us."

Polanski nodded. "He still doesn't let any of his enforcers directly under him get too big. He can't trust any of them. A gangster starts showing some chutzpah, maybe starts thinking about taking over the operation, Nasser puts a bullet in him. Fariq and the rest of them are still the same way. Probably why we're seeing these little operations splinter off."

"And our stocks?"

"We just got a shipment in from Francois. Mauser rifles. Old, but still in good condition. Grenades. Four machine guns with ten belts each. All of the detonator cable we'll ever need. And Francois' made good. They're in the garage. I've got my people rigging it out. And we've got more on the way. You've seen the bill for it."

Herzl took a gulp of his coffee. "It's good. Doesn't much change the overall picture. We're still under siege in our own neighborhood."

"So long as we keep the Muj on their back foot all the time, we've got a balance in the neighborhood," Polanski explained. "Every bit helps."

"Good," Herzl replied. "Weissman, how are the accounts?"

"Revenues are up across the board by ten per cent. That last shipment from Francois barely put a dent in our accounts. Our fish are getting more lucrative all the time. We're still paying through the schnozz to get around Nasser's blockades. But we can afford it."

Herzl nodded. "We've come a long way since the old days."

"Thanks to you, boss," Weissman said.

"No, I don't think so," Herzl said. "You know what they say? Get good people. Let them do what they do best. Don't get in their way. And you'll do well."

"Who says that?" Weissman asked.

"I do," Herzl said with a chuckle.

After a bit more business talk, Weissman left Polanski and Herzl alone.

"You know Weissman's skimming the books," Polanski said.

"Let him," Herzl said. "I know what he's taking. He's worth it. And if I replace him, the next guy will be worse. We're making money. And where's he going to go?"

"Suit yourself, boss," Polanski said.

"You're still living in that cramped flat with Rivkah. You should move into the one upstairs from there. More room."

"Meyerowitz lives there."

"He doesn't have kids. You've got two now. My head enforcer should live better. Set an example."

"I like to think I am setting an example," Polanski said. "We learn from the mistakes of the Muj."

"Tell me, Polanski, do you ever think about the future?"

"Always. How else are we going to stay one step ahead of the other guys?"

"Not like that," Herzl said. "Forget the Muj for a minute. Forget the rest of the boroughs. Do you think about what the Middle Eastside will be like for your children?"

Polanski shrugged. "I want them to grow up. If they manage that, we can think about the future then."

Herzl nodded. "Don't take offense, Polanski. But you've been fighting as long as you can remember. These last couple of years have been tough on you, I think. Not so much meshugass. But you're not a man who relaxes."

"That's why I'm useful to you," Polanski said.

"Very true. Very true. You've been a real enforcer for our operation. But can you lead in peace?"

"You've been spending too much time with the fish," Polanski said with a grin. "There is no peace here."

"Says you."

"The Muj aren't fighting us right this minute. But if they could get in here, they'd slit our throats."

"You think I don't know this?" Herzl rejoined. "Don't think I've gone soft, kid. But to tell you the truth, I am getting old. And a man takes stock at this time in his life."

Polanski listened.

"I came here long before you ever arrived. I had a wife, then. No kids. But a wife like you don't see around these parts. Don't get me wrong. Rivkah's lovely. But my wife was something. A real princess from Central Station.

"She never understood why I needed to come here. Why I needed to start something."

"What happened to her?"

Herzl frowned. "She left. I stayed. Gruber's shtarkes got hold of her during the war. I never saw her again. I've never been with a woman since. And I never had kids of my own.

"But I like to think I built a legacy. Do you know why I came here, Polanski?"

"I know. You told me that story long ago."

Herzl nodded. "I came for the same reason you came. This is our turf. We've always had this connection. Since before David the Butcher."

"Where are you going with this, Herzl?"

"I'm old now. I'll never see the inside of David's Butcher Shop. But maybe it's enough. We can see it from where we are. The gang is making it by alright."

Polanski frowned. Herzl poked him in the arm. He was serious.

"Hell, we've got money for flowers, Polanski. Flowers. We take care of our fish. We've got the guns to keep what's ours. It gives me nachas. It's a damn sight better than when I got here. Maybe it's enough."

Polanski frowned. "Maybe you're right."

"All of us Yids are running to this place," Herzl said. "The Butcher Shop down the street isn't just a place. It's an idea. I'm going to tell you something I don't think you know."

Polanski was intrigued. He leaned in.

"David the Butcher was a fish."

"What?"

"I'm not kidding. That's the real truth. He didn't start out as a gangster."

"You're bonkers, Herzl."

"This is the story. He was an actual butcher before he started working as an enforcer. The neighbors were starting a racket. He knew he'd get rolled over if he didn't make himself into a gangster, too."

"Don't tell the fish that, Herzl," Polanski said, shaking his head. "They'll get ideas."

"No, that's the point," Herzl said, a little impatient. "Tell 'em all. Make them understand. Maybe some of them have the idea already.

"We're part of something bigger, Polanski. Not just another gang. The Muj single us out. Well, we are different. Chosen, maybe. And it all started in this neighborhood."

He stared at the garden wall like he was looking past it right into the old place at the far end of the street.

"There's something about that place, the Butcher Shop," Herzl continued in a sort of reverie. "The closer we get to it, the closer we're getting to our roots. Back then, you could be a gangster when you needed to be and a fish when you wanted to be. It was a real power, to be both at the same time."

"You really want us to be like that, shammes?"

The boss nodded. "We need to learn from that story. Build on it. We don't need to physically own the Butcher Shop

170

to live on it. Like I say, I'll never see it close up. But it's something to think about. What it would have been like back then? How it could be now."

"That's why you're the boss. Always thinking long term. The big picture."

"Maybe," Herzl said. "But you need to start thinking about these things, Zev. We all do. For your kid. For yourself. You might be in charge one day."

"Don't talk like that," Polanski protested.

"I'm just putting these ideas in your head. One day, you'll need to act on them. You want to build a future here, you have to know about your past."

41

BOULEVARD OF BROKEN DREAMS

Sayid is a young man, now. Almost eighteen. He looks younger than his age.

Mostly, that's because he doesn't eat much. His height is below average. His belt holding up pants with little holes in them. It's notched to its innermost hole. The soles of his feet are hard like tanned leather from walking barefoot on the cracked and filthy backstreets.

He lived in his family home for a month after his father had died. He had no other family to speak of.

Sayid has skills. His father had taught him from an early age how to be a mechanic. And he read books. He told his son stories.

His father was an educated man. And he educated his son.

Before he died, he had taught him how to think. How to analyze. How to dream.

Sayid could make things. He had ambitions.

But there was a problem.

He was a fish with nowhere to swim.

Years of neglect had left Fariq's slum practically devoid of any economy other than criminal enterprise. Fewer and fewer fish had the money to buy cars, much less tune them up. All of Nasser's supplies came from the Upper Eastside.

And no one was hiring.

He'd gone over to Fariq's shlammers to see if he could join up with a gang. They laughed at him.

A fish turned into a gangster? That would be the day.

They beat him mercilessly and then left him in an alley.

Hours later, he picked himself up and wandered off to see what dinner he might find in a dumpster.

Sayid soon found that he was not alone. That was because Fariq had taxed the Muj on these streets with no regard to what one might consider a fair measure of return.

A few fish yet remained who were not wholly ruined. Out of some stoic sense of loyalty, they kept giant photographs of Fariq and Nasser on their crumbling walls.

Far more fish had ended up like Sayid over the past years. They wandered the streets. They sat in the shade of a burnt-out building. They were waiting for something.

Failed as fish, unwelcome even as the most menial cannon fodder for Nasser's street crews, they lived off the meager detritus of City life.

Hunger kept them in a constantly shifting frame of mind. They went from unmitigated rage to utter docility.

Yet always, Nasser and the rest of the Muj bosses of the Middle Eastside were able to work a sleight-of-hand trick. "See the fine streets and homes of the gang of Yids across the way? It is their fault that you live the way you do."

That got their attention.

"They are inferior to you. They are worthless. Gutless. Weak. But they are cunning. Oh so cunning."

This life of shit was not their fault.

"How can they live in that place while you sit in these ruins? The day will come when we will throw them all into the harbor as we should have done long ago."

When would that day come?

"And on that day, you will move into their streets. You will take over their homes. Our gang will rule this place."

In the absence of that final apocalyptic battle against the Yids, the Muj of these streets sat and stared. Perhaps tomorrow Nasser's enforcers would finally focus their violence on the Yids. Tomorrow, they would spare the taxed heads of the fish. They would refrain from kicking those that slept in the alleys and benches.

For now, those who waited would continue to wait.

But not Sayid.

He would not sit any longer. He could not bear to stare at the apartments across the way. He would not waste his sight on the Yids' streets with their new balconies and white stone walls and streets that did not reek of garbage.

He would not remain with the idle masses who stared and did nothing.

With no real work to do, Sayid was free to think.

He thought. And he planned.

He hated the Yids who had killed his father.

He hated Nasser and his enforcers just as much. Maybe more. He hated those who saved their bullets and lead pipes only for their own people; and when the Muj did ever battle the Yids in the streets, it was always to a humiliating loss. Why would he strive to join up with such useless tyrants?

And he hated the silent, squatting losers in the alleys, too. It was their silence that allowed the rest of the bosses to run their rackets they way they always had.

And if the angry, silent masses would not make a move, then he would move among them. He would find the ones like him. The smart ones. Perhaps even some with cash in the bank. Those who ought to have a future, but in Nasser's territory, were lumped in with all of the silent, squatting losers in the streets.

Sayid thought the whole world had conspired against him to make Sayid weak. But he was strong-willed. He would not be so ill-used.

He would take a third way. Not fish. Not gangster. Something more powerful. He saw himself as a continuation of the Muj legacy from long ago.

Before Nasser, long before the bosses of the City had ever been born, a much bigger gang had ruled the Middle Eastside. In the days when knives were the tool of the trade, the Muj stormed into the neighborhoods of Central Station and the Eastside.

That legendary mob had only ruled its vast extent for a short time. But it was able to reach its greatest extent through relentless brutality and unity of purpose.

Brutality. Unity of purpose. No love for material things, save the tools of war.

That was what was needed. It would be like an elemental force. They would be unstoppable.

174

Sayid was about to change the landscape of the Middle Eastside forever.

But first, he would go to his father's house and get his gun.

42

THE GOOD LIFE

Polanski walked in to find his wife on the balcony again. Rivkah was having her tea. Between sips, she was nursing their youngest while little Ben pulled at her ankles.

Silhouetted there, she seemed covered in a radiant glow. It was a welcome sight.

But it couldn't last.

"Get away from the balcony," Polanski warned, a little more harshly than he meant. "You spend too much time there. The Muj can get at you from a hundred windows."

"They wouldn't dare," she said. "Because you're so good at what you do."

Polanski lightened up just slightly. He picked up Ben and held him to his chest. "Strange things happening in the slums. You should spend more time in the courtyard. The Muj would have to bring an army to get past all the security there."

"You worry too much."

Polanski shrugged. "It's my job. Besides, that's how you know I care."

"I got an idea of how much you cared last night," Rivkah said. "You had lunch with Herzl?"

"The boss is getting funny ideas in his old age," Polanski said. "He's spending all his time thinking about David's Butcher Shop. Or maybe building something like it right here. The last couple of weeks, that's all he talks about. He's obsessed."

"Can you blame him?" Rivkah asked. "Give the old man his dreams. The Yids didn't come back to the Middle Eastside to live in the Citadel Hotel."

Zoe gurgled and spewed milk all over her breast and blouse. Without skipping a beat, she wiped up the mess.

Polanski wisely pretended not to notice. "Herzl can hold on to his dream. So can you. But the Muj aren't going to just hand over that place to us."

"You could take it, my warrior-prince," Rivkah said. "Just imagine it. Walking where David walked. Living there like the Yids back in the day."

"I prefer to live in the here and now. It's got me this far."

"You have no imagination, Zev. I think it would be like coming home again for the first time."

"Maybe. What, you don't like our apartment?" He grinned at her.

Rivkah smiled at him. "So we make a life where we are. Not such a bad life. But your daughter needs changing."

"Ugh," Polanski grimaced. "I'm holding Ben."

"Put him down and let him stretch his legs, then. It's your turn."

"So much for your warrior-prince," Polanski said.

"Come on," she chided him. "It's almost their nap time. When they're down, you can conquer me all over again."

"When you put it like that, it really isn't such a bad life."

43

VIOLENCE

None of Fariq's four shtarkes sitting around the table playing cards even looked up when the young man walked into the parlor.

This place was a dark den in the east end of Fariq's streets. It was a popular hangout for the local street-crews who weren't quite special enough to be granted access to the Asqua Club built right on top of the shuttered Butcher Shop. As was customary in all of Nasser's domains, you couldn't get decent booze. But the place was packed with vendors for just about every other narcotic, stimulant and downer that existed.

The kid had an old shirt stained in blood that was three years old. He looked calm. Emotionless even. Normally in these parts, that kind of serenity was drug induced.

But not for this one.

As a rule, gangsters hardly ever noticed the comings and goings of fish, except when it came time to taxing them. They lived in separate worlds. Even the molls barely noticed him.

He was even pretty much invisible to the other fish, too. No one paid attention.

At least, until now.

The gambling shlammers around the table were already feeling no pain. They surveyed their cards with blurry eyes. More than a few hands had been won where the victorious player didn't even have the best cards – just the most boisterous voice at the right time.

Sayid had not chosen this particular crew at random. They were the ones who had left him bruised and bleeding in an alley. That was the sort of treatment they meted out to any poor fish who happened to grab their attention – sometimes even the fish who paid their bills on time.

He walked up behind the closest one. He pulled his father's gun out of his pocket and shot the shlammer through the back of the head.

Brains splattered onto the table.

The dull-headed enforcers didn't stand a chance.

Sayid pointed at each one in turn. He shot them in the head with robotic precision.

The club music from the old jukebox played on.

But now no one was talking.

The shocked patrons watched as he calmly walked pulled open the jacket of the first murdered shtarke. The killer took the hood's revolver out of his pocket.

He now had a gun in each hand.

"My name is Sayid," he told them. He pointed at the ladies who a moment ago were taking turns sitting in the gangsters' laps and enjoying shots of various drugs. "You see these molls? They look nice, don't they?"

"Who the fuck are you?" the owner of the establishment demanded.

"I told you my name, already" Sayid said. "You should listen when I talk. First mistake."

He shot him in the stomach. The owner staggered back against the bar. Sayid shot him again.

He slumped to the floor, dead.

"Where was I? Oh yes. The girls. Look at them. Any man would want them. Am I right?"

His captive audience nodded slightly. They weren't sure what sort of response would get them killed.

"But they're a distraction," he concluded. "Whores. We don't need them."

He turned his guns on the four molls. He murdered each of them in turn.

All except for one.

He ran out of bullets before he got to that one.

He was now technically unarmed. But none of the fish in the room dared to move against him.

Sayid focused his attention on the remaining woman.

"You are unharmed," he observed. "You have been saved. It was meant to be. You will make an excellent bride."

She shuddered and fell to the ground, begging him not to hurt her.

"Why should I hurt you?" he said. "You belong to me, now."

He turned to the rest of them.

Six remained in the parlor, paralyzed with fear.

"My name is Sayid and I have no boss. I belong to no gang. I have no money. My only weapons are those you can see."

They listened with rapt attention.

"I have a proposal. If you join me, we will become a power in this place. We will take over this City. And I promise you that we will live forever."

"Nobody lives forever," one middle-aged man with a paunch contradicted him. He seemed not quite ready to fight. But he was too stupid to remain silent.

Sayid walked calmly up to him and struck him in the face with the butt of his gun.

The stunned man doubled over.

Sayid smashed the butt into the back of his skull. The man stopped moving. Blood seeped into the floor.

The killer did not look up from where he crouched over his latest victim. But he spoke one last time.

"There are five of you left. I only need four. Prove your faith in me."

The group of them looked at each other. One man with curly hair and a ridiculous tie was shorter than the rest. Smaller than the rest. He wore spectacles.

It would all be over for him soon.

44

DARK DAY

Nasser's basement office was musty with acrid smoke and sweat. Fariq and Assad were ushered into the room by burly, no-nonsense guards with beady eyes.

As ever, it was a dark and ugly place. Visitors could not know if they would ever escape.

Nasser did not bring his enforcers here to reward or chat about the old days. The place was purely for interrogations, intimidation, torture and murder.

"Tell me the bad news," Nasser growled. "Tell me everything."

"Four of my men are dead," Fariq said. "The bastards shot the whores, too. And a couple of fish."

"The Yids?"

Assad shook his head.

His turf in the northeast streets adjacent to the Yids was a good distance from the heart of Nasser's territory. Fariq's slum acted as a kind of dead ground between them. So Nasser let him live for practical reasons.

Assad's spotter networks were unsurpassed. And they hadn't seen anything.

"If the Yids were behind it, they've got ghosts working for them."

Nasser frowned. "Herzl has tunnels. He's used them against us before."

Assad wasn't convinced. "We thought we found them all. Herzl plugged them with concrete so we couldn't use them. But it's possible. Look, Nasser. I want to tell you the Yids did it. And that's the story we should be telling our people. But there's no proof. And it's not the Yids' style. There was nothing in there that was worth anything to them."

"So," Nasser interrupted, turning to Fariq. "It looks like you have a rival in your slum. Yet another gang. That doesn't look good for you, does it? Losing control."

Fariq protested, but Nasser wasn't having it. "One of us topples, everyone gets the idea the rest of us are vulnerable."

"It's not another gang," Fariq insisted. "This is something different. It doesn't make any sense. They shot the women. They left the drugs and the money on the tables. The only thing missing was the guns. It had to be the Yids."

Nasser shook his head. "What, the Yids couldn't use any of that haul? I knew about this before you told me. My people tell me there was enough drugs in there to get a herd of elephants stoned. Which, by the way, probably means you've been holding out on me, you deadbeat."

"The Yids probably got scared and ran," Fariq said. "They knew they'd get caught. If it was a new gang, they'd have told someone. Left a note, something. What's the point of doing something like this to make a name for yourself when you don't tell anyone?"

Nasser threw up his hands. "So what do you want? You want us to take on Herzl's crew? The last time something like this happened and all we did was threaten a blockade, those bastards brought the crooks from Central Station down on us. I'm not going to be drawn in again by your troubles, Fariq. This is your problem. Handle it."

Now he turned to Assad. "Keep a look out. If it turns out it's the Yids, we deal with it then. Only then. But we keep this internal for now."

"How am I supposed to keep dead gangsters undercover?" Fariq complained. "They're going to try this again."

Nasser smiled. "Good. You better catch them in the act, then."

45
THE KILLERS

It didn't take long for Sayid to make his mark on the Middle Eastside.

He tapped into a nearly limitless pool of followers. The Muj fish were fed up with paying the bagmen only to see their streets get worse and their livelihoods fail. Tired of gang bosses who claimed to be chafing at the bit to throw the Yids into the harbor, so long as the day of action was always put off until tomorrow. Sick of paying protection to thugs who focused all their violent attention on the ones handing over the cash.

They only needed to be awakened from their slumber.

It was a violent awakening. And Sayid required total submission. Once given, the men had only to stay focused on activities formerly only the province of made gangsters. It wasn't so good for the women. Sayid didn't have much use for them at all.

Three nights after the Fariq and Assad met with Nasser, the new force struck again.

This time, it was a brothel.

Fariq arrived at the scene flanked by his guards soon after the massacre.

It was worse than a slaughterhouse. Blood smeared on the walls. Cadavers piled on the stairs. Entrails torn out and wrapped around banisters. Small body parts sliced and unceremoniously dumped on bedside tabled.

Eleven whores dead. Five missing. Three gangsters killed in the halls. Probably after they ran out into the hallway – without their guns, the idiots.

And their weapons were missing as well.

The killers had struck in the middle of the day, before the place got too busy.

As before, neither the business proprietors nor the employees noticed anything particularly odd about the fish. They rented rooms with cash. They did not make any trouble at the door. They seemed perfectly normal.

How had they gotten away?

Fariq was furious. Horrified. Stupefied. Incredulous. Ridiculous.

So he investigated. He interrogated.

All of his salaried gangsters were accounted for. No one had seen any gangster running from the brothel.

Fariq was not known for his patience. And it was past time for subtleties.

He bullied. He threatened. He broke fingers and kneecaps.

One hard-boiled triggerman with a marginally incomplete alibi was reduced to a quivering, pulverized mass of brain-damaged flesh.

Still nothing.

"It had to be the Yids."

It had to be.

On the tenth night since the invisible enemy first struck, a shipment of heroin going through the harbor was intercepted.

One million dollars in street value of narcotics was thrown overboard into the water. The security men tagging along with the shipment were found later in a closet in the adjacent warehouse.

Their heads were missing.

So were their guns. And a cache of heavy explosives was missing as well.

Still, the perpetrators were like ghosts. Invisible. And slippery as any fish.

46
SIGNS

Herzl and Polanski looked down from the roof of the Citadel Hotel into streets that had become unknowable. Fariq's slums were as shadowy and dangerous as ever.

"Our spotters can't get into the place anymore," Polanski complained. "Too many close calls. They're taking fire. We can't bribe our way in. Something's changed."

"You think our enemies are getting ready to make a move?" Herzl asked.

Polanski shrugged. "I've boosted security at all of our choke-points. The crews working nearest the end of the street are seeing some suspicious things. But nothing too specific.

"The Muj are snooping around. And we're hearing things. Gunfights. Stabbings. It's chaos in there right now. We're not even sure who's outfit they're with."

"You think they'd be stupid enough to re-invent the Fedayen hi-jinks, kid? Didn't work too well for them last time."

"It's different this time. The violence is out of control. It isn't Nasser behind this. Maybe not Fariq either. None of the little bosses would pull the kind of shit going on now."

"Nasser stamps out any shtarke who gets too big," Herzl said. "Nothing happens without his say-so. It's him."

Polanski shook his head. "It's something different this time. Someone's shaking things up. Whatever it is, we have to be prepared for the worst. I've been talking with Weissman. Expediting our shipments. Training up our enforcers."

Herzl frowned. "If this is something internal for the Muj, let's keep it that way. They don't need a war by accident. And neither do we. The balance of forces may look to be in our favor – but you never know how the fight it going to turn out. Keep your preparations on a low-key."

"Done, shammes," Polanski said. "In the meantime?"

185

"I'm going to put in a call to our friends in the other boroughs," Herzl answered. "See if they know what's going on."

47
THE BLAME GAME

"There's no doubt about it," Fariq glowered. "It's the Yids. It has to be." He was livid.

"You still have no proof they were involved," Nasser answered. "I'm not going to war with the Yids because you can't keep your own men under control."

"No proof. I've interrogated every last one of my thugs. I've threatened them. Strangled them with piano wire. Sledgehammers, the works. Not a peep. If this was an inside crew breaking off from us, I'd know. The proof is that there is no proof."

Assad reluctantly assented. "We've had our spotters working overtime for the last two weeks and nothing. Maybe they're using tunnels we don't know about. Maybe they've just got really good at blending in with the street. But if it's not coming from Fariq's people, it's got to be the Yids."

"There is one other possibility," Fariq remarked. "Maybe it is an inside job."

Nasser was perplexed. "What the fuck do you think we've been talking about?"

"You tell me, Nasser. If you're trying to rub me out, I'll save you the time. I'm here. You've got your gun. Do what you do."

Nasser gave a wide smile. "Look who grew some balls? Fariq, if I wanted you dead, you'd be dead. A word of warning. Don't put ideas into my head."

"Well, we have to do something," Assad said. "Something big, but not too big. Not something that's going to start a war."

"There is no just thing as risk-free violence in this neighborhood, Assad," Nasser said with a frown. "If we kill, the Yids can go to war against us. And we won't get backed by the outside."

"Then we don't kill," Fariq said. "A kidnapping. A ransom. Something to show the Yids we can still cause trouble for them if they don't stop this. A kidnapping for two dozen corpses on our side in a week? We're giving them a deal."

Ever since Nasser had come within hours of totally losing control, he'd been playing it safe. He realized that now.

Even worse, now he saw this cautious attitude had filtered down through the ranks. Fariq's slum was only part of the picture. His own holdings weren't looking much better.

It was time for a sign. A token. Something to show the lower levels he was still in charge.

Nasser nodded to Fariq. "Move ahead with your plan. A kidnapping. That's real quaint. In the meantime, we'll get the rest of our crews ready. Just in case. If the Yids do want war, we'll give it to them."

48

MISSING PERSONS

Polanski didn't like any of it.

Explosions. Mysterious killings in the slums. A phantom gang. And none of it made sense.

Now, Herzl telling him the meetings with the head honchos in Central Station and the Upper Westside had turned up bupkis. Washington and Ivan had their own conspiracy theories. Big Ben and Francois couldn't even agree on their own stories.

No one knew what was happening.

What a clusterfuck.

It had been a long day of meetings. Checking in with the spotters. Getting the triggermen to step up their shifts. Touching base with the rank and file. He'd started distributing guns and ammo under the rubric of an early holiday gift.

Nothing too overt. If the Muj were up to something, the Yids weren't going to provoke it.

It had been a long day. He was tired. And it wasn't even done yet. He'd stop into his place to check his head.

But when he got into his apartment, he knew something was very wrong.

One of the dining room chairs was flipped over on its side. Sarah was crying in her crib in the next room. There was no one looking after her.

The glass balcony door was open and the clay planter had shattered.

Polanski kept low with his gun drawn, moving to the balcony.

Below, under the fire escape, a guard who was just now coming to rubbed his cracked head. Another guard still lay there prone against the gate.

The dazed one saw Polanski and pointed across the street at a car pulling up to the curb in Fariq's slum.

Polanski saw a flash of action as Rivkah and Ben were dragged into the backseat of the car by a pair of rough gangsters. The car gunned it to the south and turned down a back street before Polanski could get a bead on it with his pistol.

Polanski wasn't gong to wait for any ransom note. This had to have come from a higher level. And if he didn't do something now, he'd never catch them.

He had to do something now.

Polanski bolted down the stairs. He knocked over hoods and fish alike as he jumped down the steps to the main landing.

Herzl saw him coming through the lobby. He'd rarely seen his head enforcer actually looking worried. And that worried him.

"What's happened?"

"The Muj bastards snatched my wife. And Ben. I'm going after them."

"We'll get them back, Polanski," Herzl shouted. "But get your crew together. You can't go in there half-assed."

"You willing to go to war, Herzl?" Polanski growled at him. "We go in there full on, guns blazing, the Muj declare war. And they've got the backing of everyone outside this stinking borough. That what you want?"

His boss hesitated. It was only for an instant. But it was enough.

"Fuck it," Polanski said. "I've got no time for this. I'll go in alone, then."

"That's suicide."

"Trying to stop me, Herzl," Polanski said, sticking his finger in the boss' chest. "That's suicide."

He pushed past Herzl and bounded for the garage. Samberg was there, checking the motor on their new vehicle. "Where you going, boss?" the triggerman asked, surprised at Polanski's dead-eyed look.

"Just tell 'em to get ready."

"Who?"

"Everyone. Every last Yid who's packing a gun. And the one's who aren't... fuck it. Give the fish guns, too."

"What's going on?"

"You want the details, go ask Herzl. He's in charge. I got to go."

Polanski got on his motorcycle, revved the engine and left the Citadel with murder on his mind.

49

RESCUE MISSION

Polanski's motorcycle crossed distance between the Citadel Hotel and the invisible border of Fariq's slum.

The Muj lookouts saw him coming right away. It didn't matter. They wouldn't have time to warn their fellow gangsters.

Bullets traced along Polanski's path. They impacted just slightly behind his bike. He hurtled onward.

One hundred and twenty kilometers and hour. One-sixty. They could not stop him.

A car careened from its lane to broadside him. It was too slow. It slammed into a storefront leaving millions of shards of broken glass on the sidewalk.

Polanski braked hard, smoking his tires and leaving the street reeking of burnt rubber. He swerved to the right and kicked the bike back into gear. He zipped around shocked onlookers who jumped to the sidewalks to avoid getting run down.

He swerved around roadblocks, narrowly avoiding a head-on collision with cars and market stalls. There were obstacles everywhere. The slum was a crowded, chaotic place. It was no place for a Yid on a motorcycle.

Fariq's stronghold was just two blocks ahead. It was a two-storey walkup at a dead-end crawling with guards. The place would be impregnable to anything but an all-out assault.

Polanski didn't care.

The car with his wife and kid were nowhere in sight.

That didn't matter, either. Their boss would know where they were.

He sped up as he approached Fariq's fort.

192

It didn't take long for the guards out in front to figure out the motorcycle careening towards them wasn't friendly. The gangsters let loose with a hail of bullets.

Polanski's speed threw most of the ammunition off its mark. One round clipped him in the left shoulder. Another burst the front tire.

Polanski fell. The bike spun out, slamming into one of the shlammers and cracking his ribs.

Polanski tried to get up. He felt something slam into his back.

"Hey, look at this," he heard one Muj thug gloat. "It's Herzl's pirate. This fucker's crazy."

They gave him a traditional welcome to the neighborhood. A rain of punches and kicks followed.

The last thing he remembered before he blacked out was a shoe kicking him in the side of the head.

50
LIES

A bucket of ice water splashed in Polanski's face. It left him sputtering and confused.

Blood washed down his face and chest.

His body was wracked with pain. It seemed like every square inch of his body was bursting from a thousand harsh blows. His balls in particular were feeling quite rough. His crotch had been on the receiving end of several kicks while he was defenseless.

No broken bones, at least. Years of hard conditioning and working the streets had given him an extra layer of insulation. But he was feeling awfully raw and exposed at the moment.

"Wake up, Polanski," Fariq said, slapping him in the face for good measure. "Wakey, wakey. We need to talk."

Polanski's one good eye squinted open.

They were in a dark room with no windows.

He was bound to a rickety chair. His hands tied roughly behind him. He'd been stripped, exposing a purple mass of bruises and gashes from his head to his toes.

That was just from the treatment he'd gotten before he even got bundled into the room. Fariq was there with two grinning shlammers with beefy forearms and tight shirts. Polanski knew what was coming.

He could hear traffic in the street.

No sound-proofing.

It made sense. What was the point in having a torture chamber to intimidate the neighborhood if no one knew about it?

This was the place where Fariq's men had interrogated each other in a perverse cycling of persecutors and victims over the last ten days. No one in the neighborhood could have ignored the screams and moans of those held here.

And now the Muj had a Yid. And not just any Yid: Herzl's top enforcer.

This was going to be something else.

"I thought you Yids were smarter than this," Fariq scowled. "You weren't even armed. What did you think, you were just going to come into my office and kill me?"

"You took from me..." Polanski started.

"Well, of course," Fariq interrupted. "They're your whore and little brat of a son. But why make it personal, Yid? You should have waited. We could have had a negotiated settlement. An end to this violence. You might have even gotten one of them back with most of their limbs still attached. Not much hope of that, now."

"I'm going to kill you," Polanski growled.

"No, friend," Fariq warned. "This isn't a place for you to make threats. You're never leaving this place. And you're going to tell us everything we want to know. The only question here is how long it takes. You've been on the giving end of this sort of treatment, too. You know how this works."

"My people will come for you," Polanski said. "No matter what you do to me. You're finished."

Fariq shook his head. "You want to act brave? You think that makes a difference? Let me show you how much difference it makes."

Fariq flashed a scalpel in front of Polanski's face and slammed it down hard into his leg. Polanski grunted in pain.

Fariq left the blade in there. It stuck straight up out of the meat of his thigh.

"OK, Polanski, where are your thugs? Why aren't they bursting in here rescuing you?"

Polanski didn't speak.

"You want to know why? Because they are cowards. They're afraid of a war. But they think they can get at us. That's why you're here on your own. Stupid. Stupid. No one's coming for you, Yid."

With that, Fariq pulled out the knife. It hurt just as bad coming out as going in.

Blood bubbled up at the wound. It hurt like hell.

"Fuck you," Polanski snarled. "What have you done with my family?

"Oh, you're going to love this," Fariq said, giggling. "They're in your old Butcher Shop. And you can just guess what I'm going to do to them after I'm finished with you. You know, all that old equipment in there still works. The bone slicers. The sausage grinders. And of course, you have to tenderize the meat. See, you Yids aren't scared of us anymore. So we need to change that. Your family will be an object lesson."

"Fuck you."

Fariq shrugged. "You don't seem very scared yet. But you will be." He slammed the still-dripping blade into Polanski's thigh again, right next to the first cut.

Again, he left it there. "I can do this all day, one-eye. At least until you bleed to death."

"Lick my balls, Muj."

Fariq frowned. "How about this, Yid? I've already told you something. Now you tell me something. How are you getting your killers into my territory? Where are the tunnels?"

Polanski tried to ignore the knife sticking out at an upright angle out of his leg. "What... tunnels?"

"You Yids have been awfully busy. Thirty-six dead in ten days. And you call us savages. How are you getting your people in and out?"

"I don't know what you're talking about. The tunnels were filled in years ago. Concrete. So you shtarkes couldn't use 'em."

"Your people aren't riding in on motorcycles like you, Polanski. We don't see them. So how are they getting away? Don't tell me you don't know. Herzl's put you in charge of it." Fariq pulled the knife out again, slowly, excruciatingly. "Tell me everything."

Polanski shook his head. "No."

"Where's the tunnel, Polanski?" He slapped his prisoner in the face. He slapped him twice, harder. Polanski's eye patch came off.

"Fuck, that's disgusting, Yid," Fariq growled looking at the dark scarred-over socket where the left eye had been. "Tell you what. This gives me an idea."

Polanski had got quiet.

"What do you need that other eye for? It's unnatural. No symmetry, see? And that eye isn't going to grow back. So I've got a deal for you today, Yid. I'm going to fix up your face, free of charge."

"Don't," Polanski said. His voice was robotic.

"What was that?" Fariq asked dramatically. "You don't want me to cut out your eye?"

Polanski just stared at his captor with hatred.

"The next while's going to be hard for you, Polanski. You probably don't want to see what we've got planned for you anyway."

He leaned in with the blade.

"Stop it!" Polanski screamed. "Don't fucking do it." He leaned back to avoid the blade, just inches from his eyeball.

"What, is he serious?"

"I'll talk. I'll talk."

Fariq hesitated. "Come on, Polanski. You think I'm going to believe anything you tell me now? We haven't even started. We barely know each other."

"I'll talk," Polanski said. "I'll tell you where the tunnel is."

Just at that moment, an explosion went off four block away.

Sayid's new outfit had struck again in the heart of the slum.

A car blew up on one of the few street's in Fariq's turf not entirely overwhelmed by potholes. It took the life of the driver who had just keyed the ignition. Eight bystanders, too.

The blast was big enough that the sound was only slightly muffled for the captors and their prisoner all the way over on the other side of the slum.

The thugs in the room with Fariq immediately ran to the hall outside to find out what was going on.

197

Fariq didn't wait for confirmation. He went into a rage. He punched Polanski in the stomach repeatedly, one-two, one-two.

Polanski spat up blood and bile.

"You knew they were coming and you didn't fucking tell me? Fuck you, Yid. I'm through playing around." He grabbed the knife.

"You can still catch them," Polanski gasped. "I can tell you where the tunnel is."

"Oh, you crafty Yid," Fariq growled, barely able to contain his fury. "You fucking liar."

"If I lie, you do what you want," Polanski said. "But I'm telling you, there's a tunnel entrance at the southwest corner of the third house on Second Street."

"Where?"

"There's a fake wall. It's in the brown brick section. The one with the old stone."

"You fucking liar."

"If you go after them now, you're going to have to go in full-force. A lot of our guys went on this run."

"Why are you telling me that? You think I'm going to believe you're handing over your tactics?"

"If I lead your men into a trap, it's the same as lying to you," Polanski said. "And you've been clear about what happens then."

One of Fariq's shlammers came back into the room. "It was a bomb, boss."

"I know it was a fucking bomb," Fariq yelled. "What am I paying you idiots for?"

"What do we do, boss?"

"You stay here with this Yid," he ordered the shlammer. "Don't let him out of your sight. I'm going to get Assad. Fucking gangster better start earning his keep."

Now it was just Polanski and the shlammer left in the room.

"You boys are so fucked," Polanski warned. A smile came to his lips.

"Shut up, Yid."

"They're coming now, you know."

"I said, shut up."

"You know what, Muj? I got an idea. Why don't you go through my jacket pocket over there. The one on the left."

The thug hesitated.

"Just check it. See what you find."

He went through the pocket. Polanski's captor found a neatly folded paper. He opened it up and found what looked like a map of a building.

"You know what you're looking at, Muj?"

"What, you think I'm stupid?" The Muj gangster growled. He held up the crude schematics upside down.

It was the map of the Cairo Club Polanski had kept since years ago. He was betting that the last thick-headed, probably illiterate Muj shlammer left in the room with him was too dumb to tell the difference.

"That's the plan for this building," Polanski said. "My boys are on their way over here. They've got the same map. That blast you heard was just the start. They're coming here."

The thug looked confused.

"In another five minutes, maybe ten, they're going to come up through the basement of this place. My Yids are going to go into every room you see there. And they're going to kill you."

"Shut up, Yid."

"It's a shame Fariq's gone. I would have liked to see that shnook die in front of me."

"I don't believe you. Shut the fuck up."

"Don't believe me, then," Polanski said. "It's your life. If I were you, I'd get out of here. I'd at least check down the hall one more time. See if the cavalry was coming. But that's just me."

The shlammer shook his head. "Fuck you."

"Suit yourself."

"Twenty seconds. I'm going to leave this room for twenty seconds. If you moved an inch when I get back, I cut your fucking head off. I don't care what Fariq says."

Polanski grinned. "Deal."

The shlammer eyed Polanski warily.

He trotted off into the hall.

Twenty seconds.

Fifteen seconds.

Twelve seconds.

Polanski tipped his chair forward at a forty-five degree angle. He'd have just one shot at this.

The numbskulls hadn't bothered to bind his feet. He shot back against the wall with all the force his legs could muster.

It was all or nothing.

Like everything else in Fariq's slum, the furniture was old. Creaking. Run-down. This particular rickety chair was no exception.

The back of the chair and one of the back legs broke off as it hit the wall. The backing dug into just below Polanski's shoulder blades, tearing the skin.

He bounced forward, falling on his face. But his arms were now free.

He could hear the shlammer's footsteps pounding back.

Six seconds.

Polanski rolled to his side and tucked his bound hands underneath his legs.

Two seconds.

Polanski grabbed the chair leg with his bound hands. He rolled to his feet and lunged for the door.

The shlammer got into the doorway with his revolver out. Polanski drove the chair leg down onto the man's right wrist, crunching bone.

The gun dropped.

Polanski followed up with a crack to the man's mouth. He knocked out half his teeth and sent him crumbling into a heap by the door. A third over-the-head swing crushed his captor's skull.

Polanski pulled the body fully inside the room with both hands. He'd have to be quick.

He tore at the rope that bound his hand with his teeth. He managed to loosen the bond enough to wriggle free.

The chaos ensuing from the bomb blast had focused the Muj's attention on what was happening outside. Polanski had just the barest shot of making it out of there alive.

It helped that there was a real tunnel in the slum from the old days, from the first turf war in the Middle Eastside.

The Yids had really closed it off from their end with concrete, like he'd told Fariq.

But Polanski knew that after the war, they didn't have enough filler to take care of the entire section. The second stage in Muj territory was probably still hollow and accessible for anyone who knew how to get to it.

Polanski knew that. And he had nothing to lose.

It was time to go.

51
THE TRICK

Bibi Waldman's crew had a perfect view. They could see Assad's men coming along the narrow lane a half block down from Second Street. It was not a welcome sight.

Their lookout spot was in a fairly quiet part of the neighborhood most of the time. But it was the closest Yid stronghold to the Butcher Shop.

Their outpost was the most vulnerable of all the Yid buildings in the Middle Eastside. It was the easiest one to cut off. So Polanski made sure Bibi always got whatever he wanted. The best trigger-men. The sneakiest spotters. Guns and artillery up the wazooh.

No way the Muj were going to bust in on this place without a big army.

So Bibi was concerned when he saw a big army coming his way down the lane.

His lookouts were wide-eyed with shock. "Check it out, Bibi. We got company."

The Muj had gathered in strength at the southwest corner of the third house on Second Street. So technically, they were still on Muj territory.

But this was no ordinary gaggle of shlammers out to mark their territory. They weren't just there to thumb their noses at the Yids from across the lane.

This group was bristling with guns. At least three street crews had joined forces. Armored cars backed them up, though the sheer number of shtarkes on the street left no room for them to drive through.

"What the hell are they doing there?" Bibi asked.

Fogel, his spotter up top, was not liking what he was seeing. Some of the Muj were pressing up against the wall around the one half-stone half-brick section midway between them.

What were they looking for? The rest faced off against Herzl's territory.

"They're getting ready to attack," Fogel said. "No way this is a coincidence."

"What do you mean?"

"Polanski's family got snatched this afternoon. And now he's gone in after them."

"Alone? What is he, nuts?"

"Man's got one eye and balls down to the floor."

"What do you hear from Herzl?"

"He's just passed word down to everyone to be on high alert. And this doesn't look good, Bibi."

They could get caught with their pants down if they hesitated. "Herzl's not going to want to wait for us to get smoked out of here."

"We shoot the Muj from here, we could be starting something big, boss."

Bibi frowned. "We can't let them hit us first. You want to die?"

"We going to start a war today, Bibi?"

"The Muj are stupid enough to show themselves before they go in after us. We'd be bigger fools not to take 'em on before they cross over here. It's my order. Give 'em hell, Yids."

"Aye aye, boss."

Ten seconds later every window in Bibi's house facing the crowd of Muj opened up with machine guns blazing. A rocket fired off the roof.

Assad's heavy crew and reinforcements from Fariq's shtarke squads were blown to pieces. They didn't even have a chance to get a shot off.

That's how the third war of the Middle Eastside began.

52

SPREADING FLAMES

Nasser's men could hear the Yids opening up on Assad from all the way across the Middle Eastside.

It didn't take long for the calls to come in.

The spotter from Fariq's slum was gasping. Nasser's bodyguards slapped the nearly hysterical man around to help him catch his breath faster.

"The Yids are attacking," the spotter confirmed. "Assad's crew got hit. But Fariq is fighting back. He says they've already beaten back the Yids by the Butcher Shop. He's slaughtered them all."

Nasser felt his temper rising. "If Fariq says he's winning, we're already in trouble."

"They need your help, boss. The war's started."

Nasser felt a sickening sense of déjà vu at this sudden development.

Once more, Fariq's recklessness had drawn him into the fight.

But now was not a time to back down. If the Yids had drawn first blood, the decision was already made for him.

They could win this. They had the guns. They had the manpower. And when the Yids were all thrown into the harbor, it wouldn't matter who started the fight.

The ones who remained would remember the boss who finished it.

"Fariq says he's already got these Yids on the run?"

The runner nodded. "That's what they say."

Nasser smiled. "Tell him we're on our way. Grab your guns. We're throwing these damned Yids into the harbor once and for all."

53
A NEW KIND OF WAR

The war was on.

Herzl knew what was up as soon as he heard the ruckus coming from Bibi's place.

Polanski was gone. That was a big problem. But he'd kept on these crews for years. He'd made damn sure every last gangster from the lowest trombenik to the most scarred enforcer was ready for this day. They hardly needed to wait for Herzl's orders to come down to move into action.

The Yids had real combat power now. The first clue that this conflict was going to be different came from the war machines moving into the streets.

They weren't just armored cars. These behemoths were full on armored personnel carriers.

There were machine guns by the freight-load, cached in basements and cellars across Herzl's holdings. Rocket launchers. Mortars. Helicopters, too.

This borough was loaded down with everything except the full-on battle tanks Washington and Ivan kept by the hundreds in their motor pools.

To an outsider, the balance of forces in the Middle Eastside might have seemed to favor Nasser's gang. The Muj arsenals were even more generously-stocked than Herzl's. The Muj had their own armored vehicles and helicopters. And they had surplus shtarkes coming out of every nook and cranny.

But the management style of the gangsters on either side of this war would make a crucial difference.

Street battles would be won by seizing the initiative, always staying one step ahead of the enemy. In this, Herzl's crew seemed to hold an immediate advantage.

Finally, each side would find out what they were really made of.

In just half an hour, entire City blocks blazed were raked by heavy guns and smashed with bombs.

The war would be fought and won in the dark corners and torched streets. The fish ran for cover. As usual, the defenseless would suffer the most in the fighting.

54
TRAVELING MAN

Polanski wore the clothes of the shlammer he'd beaten to death just twenty minutes earlier. With a fedora hat tucked low over his head, he managed to slip out to the back alley slum of the Middle Eastside without catching the attention of the otherwise-distracted locals.

He did not know for sure whether his own part in this drama was what now brought the unrelenting bang-bang and explosions just a few blocks to his north and west. But it was a welcome diversion.

It would take a war to give him the slimmest of chances to make it to his wife and child.

"Get out of the street!" one shlammer running near him from a dark alley shouted. "The Yids are on their way over here!"

As the hood got near enough to possibly recognize something amiss with the traveling man, Polanski shot him full in the face with his stolen revolver.

He kept going, making a beeline for the dark alley. No one else would see him go.

Polanski found what he was looking for. There was a door in the alley about halfway to the end of the path to the south. This building had not been here, years ago. It was recent construction.

But with any luck, it would have what he was looking for. He knocked on the door.

A shtarke with a suspicious look opened the door just a crack. "What the hell do you want?"

Polanski shot this man in the forehead.

He entered the apartment. Another of Fariq's henchmen came down the stairs.

Polanski emptied four bullets into him.

There was no further movement inside the building.

Outside the air was filled with the sound of guns and bombs. Shouting. Screaming.

Polanski smiled.

By this point, he was operating entirely on instinct. He was an intruder. Every sentient being in this part of the Middle Eastside would exterminate him on sight.

So there was no option but to keep moving. Keep killing.

He had to hope that the battle outside would distract the Muj for a few minutes.

As it turned out, the Yids were proving to be more than a mere diversion.

55
TRUTH AND LIES

Three hours after the war began, Nasser was being fed a steady stream of unmitigated bullshit.

"The bodies of the Yids are piled up high from the west to the east," Husayn jubilantly reported to the boss of bosses in the Middle Eastside. "Eighty vehicles totally wrecked. The cowards are leaving their weapons behind and running for cover!"

"How many dead?" Nasser demanded.

"Two hundred!" Husayn declared triumphantly. "We have eyewitness reports coming in from all over the Middle Eastside."

In fact, he had no numbers to corroborate this fiction.

Precisely eight members of Herzl's crew had been overwhelmed by firepower. But the buildings they were defending remained in their gang's hands.

Civilians weren't so lucky. Many of Herzl's panicked fish running for their lives had been cut down by indiscriminate fire. It didn't matter to the Muj whether they hit gangsters or bystanders. They were all Yids.

The Muj street-crew leaders bolstered reports of their great achievements. It was an old trick to secure greater rewards when the latest outbreak of violence was done.

Husayn's misinformation owed something to that tradition. But Husayn was not a particularly incompetent or unreliable gangster. He was actually quite typical for a Muj henchman risen high in the ranks.

Years of purges and summary executions of any enforcer deemed powerful enough to give Nasser a run for his money had delivered predictable results. His gangsters were utterly incompetent when fighting those who could fight back. Yet they were also pathologically allergic to reporting failure – to the point that Nasser's perception of reality from the basement of his headquarters was divorced from anything resembling the facts on the ground.

Nasser knew his men were lying to him. He was skeptical. But part of him wanted to believe.

"How much turf have we taken?"

"Three square blocks," Husayn reported. "And six more are on the verge of falling. Fariq alone has captured an entire street."

In reality, Fariq's crew had been entirely left to their own devices. Fariq himself was nowhere to be found. The few thugs under his command who had actually thrown themselves into the fight rather than holing up in their bunkers were already dead.

Nasser didn't know any of this. Maybe he didn't want to know. "Get the hoods guarding the Asqua Club. I want them in the fight."

"Boss?"

"You heard me. There's no need to hold them back anymore if the Yids are folding."

"Yes, boss."

Meanwhile, the situation in Herzl's office across town was a study in contrasts.

"What the hell are you talking about?" Herzl roared at Eban and Tovey. They had barely even started their briefing. "You think I was born yesterday? Give it to me straight."

Eban shrugged. "Boss, I don't claim to understand. I just know what I'm seeing with my own eyes. The Muj are committing suicide out there."

"What about Polanski?" Herzl said. "Have you found him?"

"He's still missing," Eban said. "His family, too. We're still searching."

"Keep at it. Now give me the numbers."

There were now over two hundred confirmed kills among the Muj street crews, from the lowest-ranked shtarke to the crew bosses themselves.

Three helicopters taken down. Forty vehicles burnt to scrap. That included five fully decked-out armored personnel carriers shipped in from Ivan. Four Muj city blocks overrun, including Fariq's safehouse.

Herzl couldn't believe his ears.

He wanted to. But he just couldn't trust the numbers.

"It's like this," Tovey explained. "We're shooting from the buildings. The Muj are coming at us from the streets in waves. It's like they're robots or something."

The Muj street bosses were urging their men forward at gunpoint; that is to say, the bosses had their guns trained on their own men's backs, not on the Yids. Trapped between their bosses' guns and the Yids' overwhelming firepower, the rank and file were getting killed out there.

"We wipe them out from our positions," Tovey said. "And they send in a helicopter. We blast that out of the sky. And then another wave of idiots comes at us. We take them out. And then a troop carrier. And none of it is coordinated!"

"It's like they're stoned," Eban said.

As it happened, that was yet another problem plaguing the Muj offensive. Muj gangsters had epidemic rates of addiction to smack to help them get through the drudgery of life in Nasser's territory.

Given the nature of their tactics, it was probably just as well.

All strategic nuance from the Muj side boiled down to a single word: "attack". This is what happened when a top boss had relegated everything to go through him. The street crew leaders were worthless.

In a real fight, that kind of idiocy cost lives.

In this case, it was costing a lot of them.

From Herzl's side, if Polanski were leading the battle, he'd have ordered his crews to go for the enemy's throat by now. They could finish the war fast.

But the boss was more cautious. That was always his way.

"Keep up the pressure on the Muj. If the crews can hold turf, they should take it. But I'm not going to risk everything."

Eban frowned. "What about our crews to the south? They've got a bee-line to the end of the street."

"Tell them to hold off on attacking near David's Butcher Shop. We'll leave that for last."

"As you say, boss." They weren't pleased at being told to keep back. But there was a chain of command to follow.

The war went on. But the Yids and the Muj weren't the only ones interested in the outcome of this fight.

As Herzl finished his briefing, ambassadors from the other boroughs closed in from the north. They flew in towards a neighborhood that once again threatened to upset the balance of power in the City.

The outsiders could not let this go on.

56
THE TUNNEL

In the basement of the building where he'd murdered three men, Polanski found what he was looking for.

The tunnel was right where it had always been all these years. Herzl had shown him the maps of the sections. Polanski had a good memory for them.

There were no new tunnels built since the first war with the Muj. They'd blocked off those ones to prevent their enemies from using them.

But Polanski knew where he was. He studied the maps of the Middle Eastside almost every day. Herzl's enforcer was always looking to etch some small advantage out of the lay of the land. And in the basement, underneath the floor, he knew he'd found it.

The dumb Muj must have thought the area beneath the hole on the west side of the floor was an ordinary sewer. No plumbing lines ran to it. But they were gangsters, not plumbers. So they hadn't figured it out.

Polanski pulled the cement cover off and rolled it to the side. A simple metal grate was all that was left between him and the tunnel.

Polanski rummaged through the house until he found something approximating a set of hardware. There was a short crowbar-type tool that would come in handy.

Six minutes of prying and lifting later, he was in.

Polanski wiped his brow.

He was covered in sweat and blood; some from him, some from his victims.

The initial adrenaline from his escape was wearing off. Now waves of pain were washing over him from the beating and torture he'd received at the hands of the Muj. His leg wounds, now bandaged, were particularly unwelcome. He was not looking forward to crawling sideways through a dark tunnel. He felt utterly wrecked.

But his wife and child were waiting out there.

He had to do this.

There was no easier way to get close to the Butcher Shop. Crossing on foot through the back alleys of Fariq's stronghold for three blocks, he was bound to get clipped. So he had to go underground.

It was dark down there. But he'd done this kind of thing before.

Back in the day, he'd crawled through sewers with shit and piss and rancid things he couldn't even identify partly blocking his way.

He'd done it starving. Hurt. Half-mad from waiting in silence for days on end. Waiting for the moment when Gruber's men would come for them and finish off the last of the Polanski crew.

But he'd survived.

And now, as he crawled forward, he had more than himself to think about.

He wasn't planning on a heroic rescue. It wouldn't be like the daring prince slaying a dragon to save the virtuous princess.

More like man shoots fuckhead dead, stomps on his corpse.

That would be good enough. Nobody read fairy tales in the Middle Eastside, anyway.

He thought about that as he crawled though the dark tunnel.

57

LOSING IT

Above ground, Fariq looked just about ready to snap as Husayn gave him the news.

"Send my crew into that mess?" Fariq shouted, pointing at the maelstrom of gathering flame and gunfire that was pouring into his territory. "On whose orders?"

Husayn was jubilant. "It's the big boss, himself. Nasser wants you and your men to join the fighting. We're beating the Yids. He thought you'd be pleased."

Fariq kept pointing at the chaos mere hundreds of yards to the north. "Tell me, look over there, what do you see?"

"We are beating the enemy."

Fariq was given to his own delusions of grandeur. But Husayn had him thoroughly beaten in the self-deception department.

Being the latest and closest liaison for Nasser after a long string of murdered predecessors would do that to a man.

Still, there was no disobeying a direct order from the top.

"Take them," Fariq relented, waving his hand towards the shlammers who graced the balcony, looking stupefied at the battle closing in on them. "Muj, you heard the man. You've been formally commandeered by Nasser. You are in his hands."

"You're not coming with them?" Husayn asked. "Nasser would want all of you to go and fight. Don't you want to be part of the final victory?"

Fariq stared at Husayn with utter contempt. "The boss would want someone to stay behind and guard his most prized Asqua Club. We're not going to let some sneaky Yid get in here and plant a flag on the roof because we abandoned this prime real estate."

"He didn't say anything about that."

"Our enemies are cunning, Husayn. Don't forget that. Besides, we have hostages downstairs."

Husayn looked perplexed. "Hostages? Now that we are at war, Nasser has ordered the execution of all prisoners."

"You fucking twit," Fariq snarled, slapping Nasser's envoy. "I am still in charge here. Take my men down there to get into the great Yid beat-down. Go to it. I am staying here. If Nasser wants to make me go, too, he's going to have to order me himself."

Husayn looked dumbfounded. "I will tell him what you said."

"Go fuck yourself."

Fariq's remaining personal crew went down to mix it up in this latest gang war.

They'd all be dead or scooping up their own guts with their hands in less than two hours.

Fariq went down to the Butcher Shop where he was keeping his captives. If the war was going to end well for the Muj, he would have to take brutality to a whole other level.

That was the only way their enemies could be made to understand.

58
HALTING ORDER

The helicopters landed on the roof of the United Hotel. The esteemed ambassadors and their guest of honor were escorted into the gilded dining room as quickly as etiquette would allow.

This place, with its ornate glass, gleaming silverware and thousand-dollar champagne bottles was a surreal oasis from the chaos of the Middle Eastside. Under normal circumstances, Herzl would be pleased at taking part.

Right now, he was furious.

He couldn't say no to the movers and shakers of the City. And at least Nasser was so impossibly holed up in his bunker that he would not be able to attend this session for practical reasons.

But still, this interference couldn't have come at a worse time.

"We demand the Yids pull back their forces from the Muj neighborhoods to the full extent of the old status quo," shouted the non-aligned shlammers of the Eastern districts. Ivan was there, egging them on every bit of the way.

Washington and the bosses from Central Station were at least willing to concede that a ceasefire might be premature. It wasn't yet clear which side had started this latest flare-up. And Big Ben and Francois were still steamed at Nasser for having the temerity of surviving the last war (even if it simply wasn't practical to express that same sentiment to the powerful boss from the Upper Westside).

"This latest outbreak of violence is just going to end up hurting us all," Washington said.

"This isn't about you," Herzl insisted. "The Muj aren't knocking on your front door."

"Look, Herzl. I don't have the facts about who started this latest round of bloodletting between you and the Muj. And

217

I know Nasser's been twitchy lately. But it doesn't really matter who started it. This has to end."

Herzl would not back down. "That's what I'm trying to do. You've pulled me away at a very delicate time. This whole meeting is ferkakdeh."

"We did not make you one of us so you could act like a mad dog, Herzl," Ivan shouted. "There are rules in this City."

"I know all about your rules," Herzl insisted. "But it turns out my gang is the only one that really has to play by them. The rest of you hypocrites get a pass."

"Arrogant upstart," Ivan growled.

"With all due respect, Ivan, your intransigence isn't helping matters," Washington interrupted. "If you hadn't flooded the Middle Eastside with guns, we probably wouldn't be in this situation."

"You think you're the boss of me?" Ivan shot back. "Get a handle on your attack dog, Washington."

"Don't push my buttons, Ivan," Washington snapped.

"Maybe we should just let the cards fall where they may," Francois added. "Who knows? Maybe we'll get a better result this time."

"Who's winning?" shouted the gangs of the East, in unison. "That's what matters!"

"Oh, shut up," snarled Big Ben. "We all know which side you're backing."

"All of you, shut up!" Herzl commanded. The rest of the gang bosses were shocked into silence. "You're all acting meshuga. I'm in the middle of a war. And I have to make time for you lunatics? Feh. I've leaving."

"You can't!" the others shouted. "We haven't decided what we want yet."

"Try and stop me," Herzl warned. He started walking out.

"You've got 'til sunrise," Washington announced, ignoring the catcalls and heckling of bosses who thought they'd been shunted aside. "Sunrise, Herzl! This war is no good for anyone. End it."

"You heard your boss, Comrade Herzl," Ivan shouted. "Sunrise. Or the real powers in this City are going to show you Yids what war's really like."

"Enough of this," Herzl snarled back. "I'm the boss of a gang that is equal to any of you. And I have responsibilities to take care of."

The boss of the Yids was ferried back to the Citadel Hotel on a helicopter at full speed.

Soon he was back on his own ground, overlooking the scenes of open war in the streets.

Tovey was there to brief him and take orders. But Herzl could barely hear him talk. They had a new and arbitrary deadline in place.

Hoping their temporary advantage would hold, there was only one order he could give. This war had to change the status quo. They had to make it so the Muj were beaten, decisively, in a way that no one could possibly dispute. They had to be utterly wrecked to stop this up-down random cycle of destruction. And they had to do it in a way that no outsider could reverse by fiat afterwards.

Herzl's hand was forced. They had to go for broke.

"I want you to put all available forces down this street and take out the Butcher Shop. No heavy artillery. We want it intact. But do whatever you have to do. And one more thing."

"What is it boss?"

"If you don't get it before sunrise, we're fucked."

59

THE TRUTH HURTS

Nasser emerged from his bunker for the first time in years.

The smells of war were a shock to his system. There was smoke from burning gasoline. The stench of burning rubber and human beings. The fires were out of control.

This was as it had been in those dark days of the last conflict. It was like it had never stopped.

Only now, it might be worse.

The rat-tat-tat of ten thousand bullets from guns spanned all sectors of the neighborhood. It was a shocking cascade of percussion. Explosions rocked the streets all around.

He looked up and saw one of his prized helicopters struck by some kind of missile. It exploded mid-air. The wreckage flared off in every direction.

He'd come up to see the final victory of his forces over the enemy. Instead, his own senses told him he was witnessing a rout.

Husayn was just pulling up to the bunker again on a motorcycle as Nasser came out. He was smiling, practically wild-eyed with exuberance.

"Greetings, boss," Husayn shouted over the sound of whizzing bullets and the impact of incoming mortar rounds. "We are winning the war!"

"What did you say?"

"Our elite forces from the Asqua Club have joined the fight. We will surely drive the Yids into the harbor before the night is through."

Nasser smiled sweetly as his eyes narrowed. "Fariq is with them, then?"

Husayn shook his head. "He has chosen to stay and guard the Club on his own. What a brave enforcer for you, boss. It's a shame there are not more like him among us."

"A shame," Nasser repeated, again answering in a sugary voice. "Yes. It is a shame. Look over there, Husayn. How would you say we are doing?"

Husayn looked at the fires and tracer rounds of the battle getting closer.

The middle floors of one building exploded with the impact of incendiary bombs launched from a truckbed a few blocks out. The building collapsed moments later.

They could hear the panicked cries of Nasser's forces retreating from a relentless volley of shelling. The advancing enemy might be outside the bunker in minutes.

"Our gang is on the verge of beating these Yid bastards once and for all, boss. It is all because of you. You are our brave commander."

"And your loyalty should be rewarded," Nasser said.

While Husayn was still looking the other way, he blew the henchman's brains out.

Nasser fiddled with the clutch of the motorcycle for a few moments. It clicked into gear and the engine fired up.

He gunned it at full speed for the Asqua Club.

60
PATH TO VICTORY

Polanski felt the cool night air on his face about ten meters from the end of the tunnel.

For a little while there, he felt like he was already dead in the dark. Maybe he was doomed to crawl in the hole forever; always in the dark; always in pain; never quite able to reach his family.

A grate overtop led to a back alley of the street adjacent to the Butcher Shop topped by the Asqua Club. He looked up.

It was night outside, but something weird was going on out there.

Flashed of light burst the darkness for moments in time, dissipating, then came back even stronger. In his broken-down state, he didn't immediately connect the light effect with the racket of bombardment that now echoed through the tunnel.

There was no time to admire the fireworks.

The next part was going to hurt.

So what else was new, Polanski thought. He braced his back against the grate and pushed up against is using all the last force in his legs. His raw bloodied right leg screamed at the affront.

Waves of entirely new pain ripped through him as the grate dug into his back.

The grate popped up. It wasn't bolted down, luckily enough. But it was heavy as sin.

It took a full six minutes of back-breaking heaving and lunging for Polanski to get the obstacle out of his way.

Polanski poked his head up. The street was deserted.

There wasn't even the traditional congregation of Muj shtarkes at the balconies and other choke points around the building. Bizarrely, the place looked... abandoned.

A heavy explosive round burst at the side of a building about half a block north.

Retaliatory automatic fire from the windows in that structure and the building across the street seemed to hold back whatever forces were coming this way. Still, it was nice to see his colleagues had made such progress.

It was war after all. And it seemed to all be playing out on Nasser's turf. That was just swell.

Hoping against hope that the Muj defenders in this neighborhood would remain focused on the main threat, Polanski rolled out from under the street and into the alley.

He kept low as he ran. With no vehicle, there was nothing to it but to keep moving on his own mashed-up legs.

The last twenty feet seemed like a mile.

At least one of the Muj in the adjacent buildings had spotted him. Bullets ripped up the street around him as he got halfway.

Blind luck and poor marksmanship were the only things saving Polanski from an ignomious end so close to his objective.

Mercifully, the gunfire from the building ended almost as abruptly as it had begun. Polanski would never know if that was the result of a gun jamming or an astute Yid taking out the sniper.

But the end result was that Zev Polanski would be the first Yid to so much as touch the wall of David's Butcher Shop in many generations.

Now he just had to look for a way in.

He saw it almost immediately. A stairwell up the side of the building that led to a padlocked door. It had to lead somewhere.

It was a big lock. But that's what shotguns are for. And he wasn't going to be kept out of this place now.

61

ONE HOUR TO DAWN

Eban led the assault. It moved inexorably southward past Bibi's stronghold. At the end of the street was the Butcher Shop.

The Muj had ceased their wave attacks when they ran out of enough gangsters to form a decent wave. Now the last goons had fallen back to a more conventional fighting strategy of actually shooting from covered positions.

It was slowing the Yids' advance, but they were still moving forward with workmanlike tactics: blast all visible Muj gunmen with overwhelming force from a distance. Send the crews into the buildings to engage the last defenders right close up and personal with grenades and shotguns. Keep shooting until the enemy stopped shooting back.

"Machine gun at eight 'o' clock, balcony, half-left," called the spotter on top of the armored vehicle. The gunner glanced him and raked the target with fifty-caliber ammunition.

Machine gun and gunner both disappeared into a mist, along with the balcony itself.

The gangster at the helm was loving it. All shlammers love guns, the bigger the better.

And with this latest outbreak of hostilities, the Yids were trying out all of the great toys Polanski had shipped in over the years.

Thanks to the Muj' ridiculous tactics and inability to adapt, the Yids were making good progress. Nasser's forces kept fighting like morons until their last dregs were forced to adopt methods beyond running suicide missions at gunpoint. Now those last dregs needed to be cleared.

But it was taking time. And it was already four 'o' clock in the morning. The first glimmers of dawn would be coming up in an hour.

Eban took up a pair of binoculars and scanned ahead to the building at the end of the street.

Not much movement down there, but what the hell was that moving in the street?

He focused the binoculars to catch a figure moving in the shifting fiery light of the street. There was someone creeping towards the Butcher Shop.

For just an instant, he managed to sneak a glimpse of the man's face as he looked back towards them.

Polanski.

No doubt about it. The eye-patch. That stance he'd often seen, training up-and-coming trombeniks to approach their target without being seen, before slitting their throat.

It was definitely him.

"Looks like we've got an inside man," Eban shouted down to his crew. "Polanski's at the Butcher Shop."

The rest of the gang was incredulous.

"How the hell did he beat us there?"

"I thought that cocksucker was dead for sure!"

"Where'd he come from?"

Their celebration was cut short by a rocket streaming down from the roof of a five-storey walk-up.

The round hit the street just to the side of the personnel carrier. It exploded, taking out two of Eban's men in a white flash.

The impact rocked the vehicle, nearly flipping it. The carrier crashed down with a shock that compressed spines.

But they weren't dead yet.

The Yids returned fire.

Meanwhile, automatic fire sprayed at them from the other side of the street. Bullets popped off the side of the hull.

Eban felt the wave of heat roll past him. He was still alive. Shaky with adrenaline, he called out the order.

Two 'o' clock. Rooftop, half right.

Fire.

They had a lot more business to finish before they'd get to the end of the street.

But the sun was just a sliver of darkness away from coming up on the Middle Eastside.

It was going to be very, very close.

62

DELIVERANCE

Polanski's blood froze as he entered the building. He could hear the mad shrieking of his wife's tormenter somewhere in the building.

"Don't black out yet, bitch," Fariq's voice carried through the back halls of the Asqua Club that the Muj had built over the Butcher Shop. "It may hurt now. But you black out and that's when I turn my attention to your kid, understand? You'll want to be awake for this!"

Where the fuck was Fariq's voice coming from?

Polanski threw down the empty shotgun and switched over to a pistol he'd picked up back at the house. He moved forward as fast as he could. His aching body lumbered forth.

It was hell. His wife and child were somewhere in here with an absolute maniac who had already done who knows what.

But it was dark in there. The Muj could be around any corner. Where the hell were they?

He couldn't find a direct route to the voice that echoed off the walls. His mind raced. There was cold inside him.

Rivkah screamed.

Benjamin sobbed uncontrollably.

Polanski's heart fell.

"Come on, woman," Fariq shouted. "I haven't even cut you yet. You're scaring your kid."

Polanski searched the main lobby of the Club. Nothing. Where was it?

"This has to last, you know," Fariq started in again. "I have to do something real special here. You know the war's going to stop soon. It always does. We'll be back to the same-old, same-old. So we have to change things. You Yids are going to be scared straight. You're not going to fuck with us any more."

Polanski followed the voice.

It didn't make sense. No doorways to get to it. Nothing. Wait. The floor.

"Get away from me with that!" Rivkah shouted. "I swear, I'll fucking kill you."

Polanski saw it: a trap door behind the bar.

"You've got spirit, bitch. Like your husband, before he died."

"Fuck you."

"I'm going to enjoy this."

Benjamin cried his two-year old lungs out.

Polanski yanked the door open. It creaked. But there's no way anyone could have heard it over Rivkah's screaming.

There were steps that led down and turned to the right. No time to be subtle.

He leapt to the first landing.

Rivkah was caught between gagging and screaming now.

Fariq laughed.

Polanski pivoted, leaping down the second set of stairs to the concrete floor.

His injured leg gave out part-way. The pain was awful.

But he couldn't stop, now. He kept going, staggering forward.

There he was. His pistol aimed at the bastard who was caught in the middle of trying to saw his wife's arm off with a serrated bone-knife.

A whole set of butchering implements were ready for action.

Rivkah was blindfolded. She was tied faced-down to a cracked stone carving table. Her face was bruised. Her clothes torn.

Now her fresh blood dripped on to the floor. She screamed bloody murder through gritted teeth.

Benjamin was out of sight.

With any luck, he was hiding his eyes from the horror.

Polanski's eyes were wide. His heart was filled with hate. His arm stretched straight out. The pistol was an extension of his hand. It all seemed to take an eternity.

228

His finger pulled the trigger.

The gun fired.

Fariq's focus was entirely on the object of his torture. He was utterly trained on his work. In his own mind, this was just the beginning of a long night that would go down in history. He never even saw Polanski coming.

The blood spurted out from under Fariq's left collar.

His eyes went up.

A second shot took flesh off the side of his neck.

He fell back behind the butcher block. The saw that had dug into Rivkah's flesh clattered to the floor.

"Zev!" she shouted, still blinded. "Zev, is that you?"

Polanski staggered forward. His throat had constricted. He couldn't speak. But he moved toward her.

Fariq popped back up. His shirt was stained red from his neck down to the waist. His eyes were like a mad dog's.

He held Benjamin in his right arm around his waist. Polanski's son was straight between him and his adversary.

"Drop... the gun, Yid," Fariq warned, shifting from side to side, keeping the wailing Benjamin firmly in hand.

Polanski kept moving forward. His legs were ready to collapse. His body was still wrecked from his earlier treatment at Fariq's hands.

But he would not go down.

"I said... drop it," Fariq warned. He put his right hand on top of Benjamin's head and made it clear he had the power to break his son's neck with a single sweep of his arm.

Benjamin gurgled, half-choked against Fariq's palm.

"Shoot him!" Rivkah shouted. "He'll kill us all!"

"Shut your mouth, you filthy Yid bitch!" Fariq shouted. "Last warning, Polanski! I'll kill your kid!"

At the sound of his name, Polanski stopped moving.

It was like he'd been called back to some nightmare reality. Something in him hesitated.

He would not put the gun down. But he would not pull the trigger.

The sound of a door latch on a metal frame loudly unlocking distracted everyone in the room.

It came from the opposite side Polanski was on, from what he realized was the main entrance to the place.

The door swung open.

It was Nasser.

"What are you doing here, boss?" Fariq squeaked. He still held Benjamin, but now moved to the side, evenly away from both Polanski and Nasser.

"There's a war on," Nasser answered. "And you know the one thing that's sure to get a man killed in war?"

"What's that, boss?"

"Insubordination."

Nasser shot Fariq from eight feet away with his pistol.

Two bullets went into his lieutenant's temple.

The shlammer crumpled.

Benjamin thumped to the floor, his eyes hysterical at this new bogeyman. By this time, the kid had lost his voice.

Polanski had his pistol pointed at the Muj boss of bosses in the Middle Eastside.

Polanski's head was killing him. His vision had started to go blurry from the pain. He couldn't focus. His trigger finger seemed somehow disconnected from his brain.

But he kept his gun up, all the same. He was ready to take the shot.

Nasser ignored him. He looked on the scene before him in the old Butcher Shop.

He knew this place. His own father had shown it to him years ago when he was a child. He never came here as an adult. It was enough to own it.

He knew the stories of this place. The history of it. The meaning of it, for all the gangs of the Middle Eastside.

He looked from the kid to the man with the eye-patch pointing the gun at him, to the woman tied down to the table with an awful gash on her left arm, to the bloody bone-saw on the floor – and back to the man with the gun.

"You are Yids?" Nasser asked to no one in particular.

Polanski's voice came back. "That's right," he uttered through gritted teeth.

Nasser nodded.

"It figures," he answered.

Then he pointed his gun at his own head and pulled the trigger.

A thick blood spatter appeared instantly on the wall to his left.

Nasser fell to the floor.

The boss was dead.

Benjamin ran over to his father and clung to his leg, bawling his eyes out. Meanwhile, his father undid the knotted ropes holding his wife to the butcher's block.

She looked rough, with a split lip, puffy face and probably at least a couple of cracked ribs. She cried as he consoled her, telling her they were safe now; that nothing could hurt them. The family held each other, crying and balled up in an embrace.

Only now did the reality of the war outside intrude on their consciousness. The sounds from the bullets and bombs outside from the battle raging around the Butcher Shop were dying down as the first figments of the dawn spread light fingers through cracks in the shuttered windows of this ancient place.

Within minutes of Nasser's suicide, the gunfire had died down to nothing. The silence was awful. Deafening.

"What's happening outside?" Rivkah asked. She'd bandaged her arm with a section of her shirt. She held Benjamin close.

He sucked his thumb, alternating between tears and an exhausted sleep.

"Herzl's gone to war," Polanski said.

"I hope our side's winning."

"From the sounds of it, we're giving them hell. But getting out of here could be rough. I don't know what it's like out there now."

As if on cue, they heard a loud knock at the door where Nasser had come through.

In the first morning light, there was a man silhouetted against the doorframe; a man with a gun.

He was just standing there. His head tilted forward as if he was searching in the gloomy light of the old Butcher Shop floor.

231

"Hey, Yids," Eban called out from the entrance. "Everyone OK in here?"

"Damn it, Eban," Polanski yelled. "I nearly shot you."

"War's over. You can put your gun away."

"Well, in that case, welcome to the Butcher Shop," Polanski answered. "Let's see if we've got something here to make some sandwiches."

63
AFTERMATH

Herzl stood on the roof of Bibi's house overlooking the Butcher Shop. He watched the fish laborers move ahead with the restoration. They were pulling the plywood off the windows and taking decades worth of garbage out from the place, piling the debris onto flatbed trucks.

You couldn't get the smile off the boss' face.

Polanski staggered up the stairs to the roof using a cane, like an old man on his last legs.

The first day after the war ended, his body felt even worse. His face was still puffy and covered in nicks and cuts. But he'd get better in time. And he was even smiling, too.

"You're up and around," Herzl noticed. "That's good. How's the family?"

"Ben's running around like nothing ever happened. Kids are funny that way. Adaptable. Rivkah's still feeling, well..."

"Shooting was too good for that fucker," Herzl said. "But your wife is a tough one."

"She'll be OK," Polanski said. "It's just going to take some time."

"Good, good."

"How go the negotiations, shammes?"

Herzl surveyed the landscape around them. Every building from here back to the Citadel and five blocks deep was pockmarked by bullets. Some places had caved in entirely from the brutal fighting. And still, a pall of dust hung over the neighborhood.

Right now, it seemed they were negotiating over ruins.

"Washington and Ivan are being putzes, as usual. But if they think we're going back to the starting lines again, they're fucking meshuga. I'm in no mood."

233

"The Muj won't settle for anything less," Polanski guessed. "And they're not going to just disappear."

"The Muj won't be dictating terms. Our boys won this war fair and square. And we both know, if the Muj won, we'd be swimming in the harbor right now."

"Then I'm glad to hear we're in such a strong position. Tell me, Herzl, what the hell are we going to do with this slum?" Polanski said with a shrug, rubbing his head.

Herzl thought about it. "Sure, we'll give back something. I don't need a million Muj running underfoot on our turf. But the big bosses from the other boroughs can't just get their way anymore."

"You think they respect us now?"

"We've come of age, kid. We're a gang that fights for its turf. If they want to dispute our claims, they can go ahead and dispute them. They can dispute them for the next hundred years as far as I'm concerned."

"You really think they'll go for that?"

"Maybe not," Herzl bragged. "But they can't just force an agenda on us anymore."

"I want to believe you're right, boss."

"If I'm wrong, you're the insurance," Herzl replied. "You and the rest of these Yids. Your son and daughter, too, when they grow up. We have a temporary advantage. But the Muj will be back. They'll build up again. And one day, when they think they can take us, we're back at it again."

"Things don't really change in the Middle Eastside," Polanski said.

Herzl hesitated. "Some things change. Something was already changing before the war. Like that bomb. The one that you say helped you get away from Fariq's prison. We still don't know who was responsible. Sure as hell wasn't us. You got lucky."

"Whoever it was might be dead, too."

Herzl didn't seem so sure. "We have no friends in the Middle Eastside. From what I hear, these ones had no scruples. Real violent stuff, even by Muj standards. And they probably went to ground in the battle. A force like that – one that doesn't follow any rules, even the law of the streets – that could be really dangerous."

"So we'll keep an eye out," Polanski said. "If there's some new outfit out there that wants to mess with us, we'll deal with them. That's the thing about being on top. Now everyone's going to be gunning for us even worse."

Herzl nodded. "You're right about that, kid. For now, we've got plenty of other problems on our plate. I've got to get back to the United Hotel for more jabber with the bosses. It never stops."

Polanski leaned on his cane. "I'll hold down the fort here, then."

"Hmmmm. Looks like you've got another visitor to keep you occupied."

He pointed to a limousine coming down the street sporting a banner with gang colours from Central Station. It was Francois' crew.

The car pulled up across the street from them and a woman got out, flanked by a burly guard in a checkered suit.

She was wearing sunglasses and a woman's suit that didn't do her figure any favors. She still looked good, though.

Justine waved to the Yids on the roof.

Herzl frowned. "What the hell does she want?"

Polanski grimaced. "Hell if I know."

64
HOME

Justine and Polanski walked on the grounds just outside the old Butcher Shop. While they talked, he admired the ruined landscape with a strange, wistful look.

She watched him closely. She was not quite sure that this was really the Polanski of her memory.

"No funny stuff, Zev," she said. "I'm here on business."

"Lady, I couldn't even if I wanted to," Polanski answered back. "And I'm a family man, now. For real."

"Good. I'm happy for you."

"So you're in charge now?"

Justine nodded. "When Francois went, they put me in charge."

"How'd he go?"

"Heart attack. He died in his sleep."

"Sorry about that," Polanski said. "So, a woman boss. That's different."

"Times are changing, Zev. And Central Station isn't like you remember it. You should see it. It's even beautiful, now."

"I believe you," Polanski said. "But I don't think I'll be coming for a visit."

Justine looked at the ground. "You've really found your place here, Zev. In these old ruins."

Polanski stared back at the Butcher Shop. "This place will look better soon. You know I never look on the bright side. But I think maybe we've got a few good years ahead of us here. Maybe enough time to really build something. Maybe something like Central Station. The Upper Westside, even."

"Keep dreaming."

"I'm serious, Justine," Polanski said. "Now us Yids have got a shot. We're taking it."

"Somehow I never really believed you'd be gone for good," Justine said. "But I believe it now."

Polanski relented a bit. "Well, who knows? Maybe someday I will come for a visit."

"You're always welcome."

"You say that now," Polanski said with a smile. "We'll see."

"I better get back to the United Hotel," Justine sighed. "They'll need me for the talks later."

Polanski nodded. "Go easy on Herzl for me. He could use a hand."

"I'll do what I can. You take care of yourself."

"We always do."

Zev Polanski went home to his wife and children in their big apartment on the west side of the street. Their new place had a great view of the Butcher Shop.

Inside, it wasn't too fancy. The furnishings were the same old dusty antiques they'd had in the old Citadel Hotel. But it was comfortable. And it was home.

EPILOGUE
2000

*

REAL GANGSTERS

Uncle Herzl was drunk.

Well, he deserved it, the old man told himself. He'd lived through it all. Stabbings. Shootouts. Gang wars. Assassination attempts. And he was still here, looking on this absurd assembly of hard-nosed shlammers and tougher molls he loved like a family. Champagne was called for.

They were all here to celebrate his ninetieth birthday in the old courtyard of the refurbished Citadel Hotel, where it had all began.

Most everyone else was drunk, too. Polanski and his family sat to the right. Benjamin and Zoe were teenagers now, seventeen and sixteen. They looked sharp in their new clothes bought just for the party. Other distinguished shlammers sat to the left.

The champagne was flowing. Caviar from the Upper Eastside. There was even a show tunes band hired from the Upper Westside. Everywhere was bright, loud, celebration.

Herzl stood for a toast. Someone clinked a glass, setting up a crescendo of spoons on wine glasses. It was time for the boss' speech.

"Ladies and gentlemen, I do thank you for coming this evening. This is really something special. It gives me nachas.

"When I came here to the Middle Eastside those many years ago with some money in my pocket, a Smith and Wesson pistol in the other and a big idea, I had a dream for us Yids.

"We'd had the run of this place once, a long time ago. Back in the days of David's Butcher Shop. But the City had been none too good to us since. We'd been thrown out of just about every decent joint in the land. Always on the run. Wandering. Never able to set up shop for too long before some other gang blamed us for some funny smell in the water. And they'd stomp our living guts out.

"So I came here with my young wife and we set up shop. I went out looking for the Yids. And they were here. Still here. Hanging on by their fingernails.

"Taxed like nobody's business by the Muj. Beaten down by the new gangs from Central Station. Murdered in the back alleys over nothing. We weren't real gangsters. We couldn't defend ourselves. We had nothing."

Herzl made a fist in his pocket and pulled himself together. "My wife left. But I stayed in this place. The Yids who were already here, they found me somehow.

"Why me? I still don't know. But we started something. We were a real gang again. We hung on together.

"And just in time, when things looked darkest, our friends, the lost Yids from Central Station came. We helped them. They helped us. We fought together.

"It's been a long road. But we got here. The Yids are united. Rich. Tough. Things aren't perfect. But they're looking better.

"You've heard the rumors. And now we're on the verge of peace. The gangs aren't fighting anymore in the Middle Eastside. Not openly, anyway. And things are looking up.

"Who would have believed back then, we'd be doing business with our former enemies? That we'd be running our rackets alongside the Muj in Nasser's old ganglands? That we'd have fish from over there serving champagne at the Citadel Hotel?"

The crowd roared their approval. The boss was having a grand old time. He talked some more. Made jokes. They honoured him with applause and laughter.

Herzl downed his glass and called for more champagne all around. The party was in full swing. The room spun with light and music and good feeling.

The fish hailing from the old Muj slums brought over the champagne.

The waiter was the only one in the room who wasn't smiling. Polanski saw him out of the corner of his eye and trailed him as he approached the boss.

There was something different about this one. Every single one of the Muj fish catering events on Yid turf had been vetted. Nothing too obtrusive, since the gangs worked pretty much hand-in-glove these days. But still, precautions had been taken.

Polanski didn't recognize this one. Not that he'd know any Muj waiter just by looking at him. But there was another kid who looked like this one. He served coffee in the courtyard every day. And that one looked almost exactly like this one. But it wasn't him.

Nearly identical. But not him.

Polanski caught the kid's eyes one last time and noticed something new.

He did recognize him after all. He knew someone who had those same eyes.

A man and his young son who lived on a backstreet in the Muj slums those many years ago. The father, an ordinary Muj mechanic. And the reckless teenager who's taken his father's gun and tried to kill him as he rode along with Justine that night.

And he remembered those eyes again, as he'd looked down on Abdi's breathless corpse. The corpse that lay there on the cold ground, only meters from the murdered body of his father-in-law.

Yes, he'd seen those eyes before.

Everyone was smiling in the room.

Everyone but this one waiter with a skinny neck and skinny wrists and an oddly chunky middle, underneath his vest.

A few others noticed as the kid came up to Herzl, like in slow motion, that hateful look in his eyes as he got within five feet of the target.

This skinny Muj kid in the waiter's vest was the sixteen year old son of Sayid. His mother was the moll Sayid had carried off on the day he'd begun his reign of terror. She lived in fear and darkness all these years. Sayid had raised this son in his own image.

Fear figured into the son's life as well. And for sixteen years, he'd been fed a steady diet of hatred.

241

There was hate for his lot in life. Hate for the slum that was his home in the Middle Eastside. Hate for the corrupt Muj gang bosses who to this day kept up their old habits of taxing and breaking anyone less powerful than themselves.

Hate for these bosses who were now on the verge of making peace with the Yids. Hate for those who lived in their fine buildings of white stone, in view of the ancient place at the end of the street.

Above all, hate for the Yids.

Those Yids. Those thieves. Those parasites. Vampires.

His father had brought up his son with nothing but hate in his heart. So there was nothing for him in this world.

Dying would be nothing for him. Better than nothing. It would be a release.

Herzl smiled and laughed as he raised his champagne glass. He laughed at some joke he'd heard long ago but only remembered just now. He rejoiced at the smiling faces of his family assembled this glorious evening.

The kid reached between his shirt buttons under his vest.

Polanski shouted. His arm shot out to protect his boss, who was halfway between him and the waiter with the eyes he knew he'd seen before.

It was too late.

The explosion killed the waiter instantly. Herzl was next.

One instant, he was celebrating a life in full. The next, he was snuffed out, his fragile form shattered into a million pieces.

Those nearest the waiter, on the other side of the table, were annihilated. The wall behind them was painted red.

Polanski was thrown against the back wall by the force of the blast. He blacked out for a few seconds.

When he came to, he instinctively staggered to his feet. His blurred vision took in the horror around him.

Polanski's clothes were covered in the blood and guts of his boss and some of the other guests mixed in. To his right, Rivkah lay on the floor, staring at him with an open mouth, utterly terrified.

Zoe was lying face down in a quickly-gathering pool of her own blood. She would be dead in an hour.

One side of Benjamin's face was disfigured in precise and symmetrical imitation of his father's wound sustained in the first war of the Middle Eastside. Shrapnel had lodged his eye somewhere between the table and the open bar. He sucked the air like a fish caught on dry land.

Blood washed over the floor.

For just the briefest moment, Polanski felt like he was dying.

He felt the cold wash over him. The darkness enveloped his heart. He fell to his knees.

With his one good eye, he looked on the world without comprehending. The world had shrunk. It became very, very small. It was just a window looking into chaos.

The cold was awful. It pricked him like a thousand needles at once. His brain went numb.

He was ready to keel over. To give up.

But he didn't. Something stopped him.

It was something that came from inside. His heart kicked in. The needles ripping into him subsided.

His mind became serene. It was so clear now.

Polanski got to his feet. He saw the chaos and the screaming. The awful truth embodied in this manic scene. Now he drank it in.

He put his hand into his jacket pocket and felt his old cool assurance coming back. The world was right again.

He knew they would get through this horror. It would take time. But they would find the ones responsible. And they would make them pay.

Zev Polanski stood there with a gun in his hand.

www.ingramcontent.com/pod-product-compliance
Lightning Source LLC
Chambersburg PA
CBHW071145170626
46809CB00002B/774